Feather in the Wind

Feather in the Wind

Shannon Buckley Moore

Quillogy Publishing

Where Words & Wisdom Meet Creativity

Book Cover Copyright © 2025 Shannon Buckley Moore.
Photograph Copyright © 2025 Shannon Buckley Moore.
ISBN: 979-8-9999750-3-4
10 9 8 7 6 5 4 3 2
Printed in the United States of America

DEDICATION

Many thanks to my younger brother, Greg, who we unexpectedly lost early in 2024. His death had a profound effect on me, and while navigating my own sorrow, I have been inspired to write. I thank him for who he was to me during our lives and who he is to me now in Heaven. For this, I dedicate my book.

Fly Free, Dear Brother.
Like a feather in the wind. Fly Free.

PREFACE

Everyone, everywhere, is looking for their "thing." Where do we all fit into this web of a world we live in?

My "thing" is writing. I have long been aware of how powerful the written word can be. You can be yourself, or you can be someone you imagine in your mind, all with the stroke of a pen. You can be where you want, when you want, and how you want. You can face things head-on, or you can escape reality. You can hurt. You can heal. You can bring your imagination to life.

I have spent a lifetime forming meaningful connections between words and using them as a tool to convince, justify, and convey everything from feelings and emotions to facts and fiction. I have done this in educational, legal, professional, and personal settings. And, among the millions upon millions of words I've written, I have still struggled with the ability to write anything of great length, like a novel.

For years, I thought I might pen an autobiography someday. I could write about what I knew. I had actually documented many short stories to that effect, but I never took it any further. Then, one day, I had a grand epiphany! I would use a few of my own experiences to *inspire* the contents of a fiction novel. This, along with my love of storytelling, led to the birth of *Feather in the Wind*.

As a side note, the cover photo is an actual photo of a magnificent Lake Erie sunset in Western New York. A year before this writing, I captured the shot as a lonely white feather floated softly through the air. A believer in unexplainable signs, I only recalled that I had taken the photo after I had nearly completed my first draft of this book. It was like the universe knew I would write this story even before I did.

TABLE OF CONTENTS

"Like a feather in the wind, we are reminded just how delicate and unpredictable life can be."

Shannon Buckley Moore

INTRODUCTION

The protagonist, Sonya Morrison, *is* the girl next door. She is you. She is me. She is a little bit of every single one of us. Also known as Sonny, Sonya grew up having hopes and wishes and dreams ... hopes and wishes and dreams that were shattered. She's had to fight battles and demons, she has struggled to heal, and she has had to overcome hurdles and recreate her life in order to survive.

She is someone's daughter, someone's mother, and someone's friend. She's a co-worker, a girlfriend, a divorced single mom ... she's a professional, a hard worker, and a military veteran. But she's also broken. That is, until her unexpected journey forces her to face her greatest fears. Ultimately, it is her courage, strength, and perseverance that set her free.

The unexpected death of an old friend brings Sonya back to her small hometown in Western New York. Along the banks of beautiful Lake Erie, it is the hometown she escaped from so many years before. It is the same hometown where she left the love of her life in the rearview mirror.

A criminal profiler by trade, her expertise becomes a critical resource to a neighboring community. Follow her as she unravels the mind of a psychopath and treks through an intriguing investigation that eventually comes full circle. Share her emotions as she tries to rekindle an old romance she never forgot. Relate to her feelings as she is forced to confront her past and the unresolved emotions tied to her former life.

Experience synchronicity—the divine order that helps things come together, even amongst the chaos in our lives. It is déjà vu, it is your gut feeling, it's your instinct … your angel's whisper. We all have these moments. But do we all listen to them?

It is through moments such as these that Sonya's story unfolds. It demonstrates the profound effect of everyday choices. It also invokes an appreciation for the unexpected opportunities, both realized and missed, that can change the trajectory of our lives.

Not your average crime story, this novel offers a profound exploration of identity, the unexpected healing through truth, and ultimately, empowerment by choice. Through surprising twists and unexpected turns, *Feather in the Wind* offers a compelling exploration into the depths of a criminal mind. Packaged as a thrilling suspense novel, Sonya's journey also serves as a reminder of the delicate balance between confronting the past and embracing the future. It is a captivating tale that encourages readers to reflect on their own personal journeys and the experiences and relationships that shape them.

"Don't just drift along like a feather in the wind. Be the choice that sets you free."

Shannon Buckley Moore

CHAPTER 1

The Call

Wednesday, June 26, 2024

Like the parting of the Red Sea, I slid the floor-length curtains to either side. The soft tan linens flowed gently aside as a welcome to the morning sun and the start of a brand-new day. The light of dawn seeped into the room, as streaks of sunbeams bounced off the crystal chandelier. The light shimmered in a kaleidoscope of colors, casting an array of mesmerizing patterns on the floor. I slid the window open and instantly heard the early morning risers chirping back and forth, going about their morning rituals. I stood there for a moment, allowing the coolness of the gentle breeze and the warmth of the golden light to kiss my cheeks.

With my face stretched to the sky and eyes gently closed, I took in a deep breath and relished in this moment of pure and unremitting peace. My trance-like state was only broken by the ringing of my phone.

As I composed myself, I lifted the phone to my ear and answered, "Hello?"

There was no response, only silence.

"Hello?" I spoke in a louder voice.

Through a slightly weeping voice, I heard a distorted female calling my name. "Sonya? Is this Sonya?"

It was clear that the caller had been crying as she sniffled on the other end of the line.

"Yes. This is Sonya. Who may I ask is calling?"

"It's Lydia, Sonya! It's me! Lydia!"

I didn't recognize Lydia through her tear-filled voice. "Oh my gosh, Lydia! What's wrong?"

Lydia cleared her throat and proceeded to tell me of the unexpected passing of our long-time friend.

"It's a terrible tragedy," she said.

I listened intently as Lydia explained that Anna's lifeless body was discovered four days earlier on one of the local beaches. She didn't have many details but had *heard* that her cause of death was an accident of some sort. The media and local law enforcement were being pretty tight-lipped at this point, not releasing many details to the public. Anna's sister had contacted Lydia to share the devastating news and Lydia, in turn, was contacting our **girl clan**. There are five of us ... or there *were* five of us, dating back to high school days. Although we haven't maintained regular contact with one another, it is an unfortunate situation such as this that would bring us all together again ... minus one.

As I hung up the phone, hot tears welled up in my eyes. One blink sent streams of heartache down my cheeks. I managed to maintain my composure over the initial shock; I was always the strong and logical one. But here I was, alone in my own thoughts. The sadness was overwhelming. But why?

Anna was the least of those that I was close to; we had a love-hate relationship. She was the "attention whore" of the group and went to great lengths with dramatic renditions in nearly every situation we were in. She was the *friend* who had to be the center of everything ... whether it be for a man's attention, on the stage, or simply among friends. Her experience was always greater than yours, her situation always more dire, and there was nothing anyone could talk about that she hadn't already experienced ... always in a bigger and bolder way. She strolled through life living off her sex appeal and theatrical performances. Too numerous to count were the male suitors and relationships, and after several failed marriages to men of great wealth, she found herself living a comfortable life.   Although Anna's narcissistic personality was at times a lot to bear, she was still a part of our little intimate group … our girl clan. I regularly reminded myself that her behavior was merely an outward expression for her incredible lack of self-worth. And no matter the negative influences she projected, deep down inside, she truly had a good heart.   The thought that a piece of our identity had so suddenly and unexpectedly slipped away, was shockingly sad. And I can't even begin to imagine what her family … her parents … must have been feeling. The realization that I was actually going to miss her, with all her idiosyncrasies, had struck me in a powerful way. My heart felt broken at that moment in time … and the tears continued to flow.

I sat down at the table. I bent my head down and clasped my hands over my face.   My dark hair, highlighted in various shades of gold, hung softly over my shoulders. Memories were swirling around in my mind.

It was in this moment that I recalled that I was with Anna when I met my first love. We were preparing to enter our freshman year of high school. It was the Summer of 1998. It was a hot summer day and we decided to cool off at the local ice cream shop. I had selected a double scoop cone with my favorite, chocolate chip cookie dough. Anna and I picked a small round table across from the entrance door where we could watch who was coming and going. I had a clear view as he walked in.

Colin Griffin. His strong, athletic build with a slightly rugged complexion caught my attention as soon as he sauntered through the door. His light brown hair looked as if it had been kissed by the sun, as it fell playfully framing his suntanned face. With a well-defined jawline, his pearly whites glistened behind a charming and inviting smile. And, as he glanced in our direction, his striking blue eyes would, by chance, meet mine. Even though it was just for a moment, it was love at first sight.

I immediately turned to Anna and as I gasped, I said, "My heart just fluttered like a thousand tiny butterflies."

It was obvious to Anna the direction I was looking and to whom I was referring. Her immediate response was to sternly reply, "You can't have him! He's mine! I saw him first!" She immediately got up from the table and headed in his direction.

My jaw dropped at her bold proclamation. I was stunned and at a loss for any type of reaction. I hadn't realized we were in competition, but as luck would have it, there would be no competition at all.

Although I couldn't hear what she was saying, I watched Anna lay her hands on her hips as she shifted her weight to one side and pushed her hip out about as far as it would go. In unison, she thrust her lily-white breasts forward and shook her head in a half-successful attempt to toss her long, dark curls over the back of her shoulders. I could see her mouth moving as she giggled and made almost embarrassing attempts to sway slowly and seductively back and forth.

"Why does she do that?" I asked myself. "I wouldn't … I couldn't," and I cupped my mouth as an amusing chuckle slipped past my lips.

This would be the first of many times that I saw her in action. The dramatic expressions on her face actually kept me entertained, but instead of captivating Colin's attention, his fleeting glances and amused grins were coming in my direction. In an astonishing turn of events, Colin put his arm forward and gently moved past Anna; he was headed straight for me.

I will never forget that day. Not for as long as I live. The feeling I had when my heart rose into my throat. I could barely speak and was stumbling over the few words that I could muster. And while everything seemed like a fog, I would always recall every single little detail from that day. The clothes he was wearing, the scent of his cologne, the look on Anna's face, and the words he used when he first greeted me.

"Hello, darlin'!" was all it took to hook me for the next six years of my life.

Thirty minutes must have passed before I was able to wipe the glistening streams from my face. "Come on, Sonya, get it together." I thought to myself as I squeezed my eyes shut and opened them again.

I traditionally kept a rigid schedule and was rapidly losing time out of my early morning routine. I needed to hurry if I wanted to get to work on time. I usually looked forward to going into work, but this was going to be a difficult day; a day overshadowed by a mix of so many emotions.

This was one of those lifetime events where you struggle with the realization that you know you should be present, but you just don't want to be there. I knew I had to attend the funeral; it was the right thing to do. But I also knew that as difficult as it would be to say my goodbyes, it would be equally as hard for me to step back into that town ... a town I've struggled to set foot into since I had left twenty years before. Reminiscing the reasons about why I had left in the first place was stirring up a whole new cauldron of conflicting feelings.

In the midst of all these mixed emotions, I was suddenly overcome by the fresh scent of lilacs, delicately floating through the air. I drew in the flowery, fragrant aroma. Closing my eyes as I exhaled, I was struck by a new feeling. It was one of bewilderment.

"That's odd," I thought. "Lilacs in July? Here in Virginia? In my living room?"

As I contemplated this thought, I recalled that lilacs had always been a big deal growing up in Western New York. Every spring would welcome the budding clusters of beauty. For a short period of time, they'd bloom abundantly. My girl buddies and I made an annual ritual out of picking bouquets fresh from Anna's backyard. How I loved that smell and this memory ignited the realization that, beyond the reason why I left, there were many good memories back home too. It was now clear that I needed to return. I cracked a small grin thinking that maybe it was Anna, giving me that gentle nudge that I needed to commit to my decision to return.

Taking time away from the office would be a non-issue. Eat, drink, work, sleep, repeat! I have banked so many vacation and sick days that I lost track of the count. This would probably legitimately explain the ruin of my marriage. My husband, Devon, or "ex-husband" I should say, always complained that I was married to my job more than I was to him. A fair statement, but in defense of myself, he also enjoyed the monetary benefits and perks of my education and hard work. He was enormously supportive of me as I pursued my educational goals. He was an amazing stepfather to my daughter in the early years, since I could never have done it on my own. And for a while, this Superman hero of mine had maintained his own very lucrative legal career. But once the boys came along, it all changed. Devon became incessantly paranoid about anyone who came in close proximity to the kids. He morphed into this monstrosity of a germaphobe. Against my own wishes, it was his decision to be a stay-at-home dad.

Although Devon hung onto a few of his legal clients, initially, we took a deep cut in overall income. In the big picture, however, my pay could still comfortably support our little family, so I was supportive of his desire to stay at home with the kids. We knew I was a rising star with the FBI and had no concerns about our financial future.

Somewhere along the way, though, I think he lost himself; he lost his self-identity. As he focused on diapers, household duties and school, he became envious of my successes. Over time, the very things that drew him toward me, were the same ones that pushed him away ... right into the arms of Lisa.

"Oh, that Skanky Ho!" I thought to myself. "The ditzy flamboyant Room Mother with double-D boobs and an ass that could stop a train."

But that's all water under the bridge. Time apart would reveal that it was a loveless marriage anyway. We had been together for all the wrong reasons. Lisa actually did me a favor and in the end, we were all able to part as friends.

Reverting my thoughts back to Anna, I wondered what could have possibly happened to her. "Some sort of accident." I thought. That doesn't really tell me much but I'm sure I'll hear all about it once I arrive back in my childhood hometown.

I knew I'd be in for a ride going back, but I don't think anything could have prepared me for the journey I was about to embark upon.

CHAPTER 2

Then There Were Four

Friday, July 5, 2024

I was jolted awake by the loud squealing sound of wheels hitting the tarmac and the voice of the attendant over the loudspeaker. "Welcome to Buffalo, New York! It is a sunny seventy-eight degrees today with nothing but blue skies in the forecast."

I sat up in my chair, returned the tray to its original position, and stared out the window as the plane coasted steadily along the runway. Anxious feelings began to arise as we cruised closer to the landing bridge. The plane came to a gentle rest as people jumped from their seats and scrambled about, trying to gather their belongings. In all the commotion, I decided it would be best to wait patiently to disembark. Good in theory, but this idle time only allowed for more anxiety to seep in.

When I felt it was safe, I gathered my own belongings and headed for the baggage claim area. It seemed uncomfortably crowded as I nestled in between the other bodies and stood eagerly waiting to retrieve my checked bag. I was accustomed to traveling and quickly learned the benefits of tying a bright pink bow on my luggage handle so it would stand out when coming around the conveyor belt. And there it was! The bright pink bow! I don't know why, but I always had a fondness for bows. Ever since I was a little girl, these delicately woven strings of fabric had appealed to my feminine side.

Clamoring through the chaos, I grabbed my things, retrieved my rental vehicle, and loaded it all in. With an hour's drive ahead of me, I was on the last leg of my journey.

Out on the open road, not much had seemed to change. Passing fields of green, open farmland, and wooded areas, all were scattered with wildflowers of every kind. This is the rural area that I had left so many years ago. Why was I feeling so anxious? Pushing those feelings aside, a part of me was actually looking forward to being back home. Not for the reason I was returning, but it would be nice to spend time with my mother, hang with the girls, and soak up familiar surroundings.

I turned the volume up on the radio to drown out whatever negative thoughts I might be having. One of my favorite songs had just come on. It was a song about survival … my theme song from younger years when I left home with a broken heart and shattered spirit. It uplifted me as I struggled to compete in a male-dominated field and became a young single mother, consumed with work, child-rearing, and continuing education. It was a motivating song that always seemed to raise my spirits. I smiled at the timing at which it aired.

Golden shafts of light came streaming through the windows, and as the warmth fell upon my face, I slid open the sunroof of my SUV rental. The slight breeze that wafted in was refreshing and it filled the space with the scents of summer that only Western New York can bring. Yes ... I was finally home.

Driving through this community of businesses, lakefront property, agriculture, and residential homes, my final destination had not been hard to find. Nestled within the confines of this small urban neighborhood stood a red brick-colored, two-story home—simple, sturdy, and strong. This well-kept, middle-class abode rose tall among the other homes that filled the tree-lined street. Its window-clad, enclosed front porch exhibited perfectly manicured evergreen bushes below. Sparsely dotted red geraniums added a touch of vibrancy and class to this simple, yet attractive home. The distinct aroma of a fresh coat of blacktop greeted me when I exited my vehicle.

Once inside, my senses were greeted with yet another familiar smell. Fresh homemade cheese pierogi's frying in a pan with butter and onions. I barely got both feet in the door when almost instantly, there were two arms wrapped around my body, squeezing and not letting go. "I'm so happy you are home! Oh, how I've missed you!"

As she pulled away, I noticed that what stood before me was a strange-looking woman. Not the woman I had remembered. This woman had a head full of gray-streaked hair and deep wrinkles that had long ago taken hold. She was shorter in stature than I remembered and as she hobbled slowly back to the stove, I couldn't help but realize how frail she appeared.

"Could I really have been gone that long?" I thought to myself.

I walked up next to this nearly unrecognizable old lady and gently kissed her cheek. "Oh, Mom. I am so happy to be here. I have missed you too!"

At her direction, I carried my luggage upstairs to the front bedroom on the right. That was my old bedroom from days gone by. The pink daisy wallpaper was still on the walls, and the pink fringe trim still lined the valances over the windows.

"She never changed it." I thought to myself.

The twin bed rested in its original corner, and the stuffed monkeys I had collected each Christmas were propped neatly against the pillow. Memories swirled of younger days when I would let myself out the window and run back and forth on the roof of the front porch. I would sneak back inside just in time for my mother to come frantically running into my room. I thought I was fooling her when I would sit quietly back on my bed, hands clasped gently in my lap. With the look of innocence exuding from my big doe-shaped eyes, I would make it hard for her to scold me. This memory brought a grin to my lips as a slight chuckle escaped my breath.

I returned to the kitchen, where we spent the next couple of hours talking like old friends who hadn't seen each other for years. Catching up on the latest gossip, world events, and of course, the kids ... all while enjoying the labors of her cooking.

"Superb!" I told her.

There is nothing like good old down-home cooking. Though it was true we hadn't seen each other in years, we had spoken on the phone nearly every day since I moved away. My mother was never one to complain and, in my eyes, she had remained just as she was when I left. But I could see that in my absence, time had not stood still.

"Have you heard any more about your friend, Anna?" Mom asked.

"What do you mean?" I responded.

My mother proceeded to say, "About the details of her death? There are rumors going around, you know? Rumors that she drowned."

"Drowned? How could that be?" I exclaimed through my surprise.

"That's what I thought too," responded Mom.

Of all the people you might expect to drown, Anna was not one of them. Her life was all about the water. She spent much of our high school years swimming her way to multiple state championships and breaking local and county school records. She was an expert swimmer and avid athlete. Even as an adult, she could regularly be found swimming laps at one of several local pools.

"That just doesn't seem likely, Mom. You know how gossip is in this small town. You know you can't believe half of what you hear."

My mom glanced over at me, tipping her chin down and peering over her bifocals. "And the other half, you **can** believe," she said.

The conversation shifted back to familiar topics. I didn't give much more thought to my mother's shared rumor since I knew all too well how these little communities can easily suck you in with their small-town gossip. Glancing down at my watch, I realized that I was running late to meet up with the girls.

"Geez, Mom, I've got to get going." I stood up from the table as I continued, "I have to meet up with the girls. But I'll be home before it's too late."

"Go! You go! We will have plenty of time to catch up! I'm just glad you're here." She said with a loving smile.

I lamented to myself, "Awwww, I just called this *home*."

I grabbed my purse and rushed out the door. It was a twenty-minute drive to Lydia's house on the lake. She was hosting a small get-together for our girl clan so we could have some time together before tomorrow's wake at the funeral home.

I had never been to Lydia's home. I had only seen pictures she had sent, but they clearly did not do it justice. Entering the beautiful estate, visitors are greeted with two massive marble pillars, both with wrought iron fencing attached to either side. The long and winding driveway is selectively lined with twelve-foot-high lighting fixtures, each with climbing clematis vining its way up their posts. The lawns were skillfully manicured and contained a rich array of local and imported flowers and plantings. As breathtaking as the entrance was, I was eager to see the view from the back. The sunsets were said to be spectacular from her patio.

Lydia greeted me at the door. She was as open and loving as always. She was the bougie one of the bunch. In literal terms, hers was self-made wealth, but she never forgot her more humble roots. With modest beginnings, she immigrated to the United States at the age of eight years old. Classy and elegant, Lydia was known to be selective in her words and was always the one to rally around the troops. Her sophisticated long, black hair and exotic look had turned many heads over the years.

Not only selective in her words, she was selective with her men as well. Everyone knew that if you were fortunate enough to be seen on Lydia's arm, you were of honorable character. After hugs and love were exchanged, she welcomed me in.

As I entered her home, I was eagerly greeted by her friendly and adorable teacup Yorkies, Miff and Maff. With tails wagging and tongues panting, they excitedly led me into the bright and open living room, where the coastal vibe was readily apparent. Surrounded by hues of turquoise and froths of white, her fondness of sea turtles and other sea creatures was abundantly clear.

In the midst of the coastal style that enveloped us, there stood Emily and Jenn. I was the last to arrive.

We were always baffled at how we all had become friends, not to mention that we stayed friends over all these years. Our personalities and lifestyles were about as different as they could get.

Emily, who stayed in a toxic marriage, accepted that she would live the rest of her days catering to her emotionally abusive and mostly drunken husband. She wasn't a whole lot better though. Too often were the times she spent reaching for liquid courage to get her through the day. And from what I was being told, those days were more frequent than not. With her children grown and on their own, she still refused to leave her oppressive lifestyle, forever declaring her devoted and unending love for the man who kept her down. Even through it all, she showed up with a smile. She showed up with support. She was always the one to show up.

Then there's Jenn. Jenn was the baby maker of the clan. Free-spirited, good willed, and endlessly naïve, she lived with her husband and six children in a converted bus on property she acquired from her parent's estate. With no use for television or internet, she spent her free time growing her own organic vegetables and homeschooling her children. She lived a low-key, hippy-style life with the occasional medicinal recreation. Out of all the girls, I think it is Jenn that I envied the most. Her uncomplicated, simple, and free style of living is one that I hadn't enjoyed since I was a child.

We all stood there for a moment, looking at one another. Without a word, each of us felt the same empty, gnawing feeling in the bottom of our guts. Instinctively, we inched toward one another until we were in one big group hug … each one clutching at the other and doing our best to hold back our tears. In that instant, the sun had gone down. We had missed the sunset and a shadow cast down upon us.

It was abundantly clear that where there once were five, there were now only four.

CHAPTER 3

Justice For Anna

Saturday, July 6, 2024

There was a stream of people as I approached the funeral home. This magnificent structure, immaculately kept, had served for many years as a historic landmark within the close-knit neighborhood of our quaint community. It was initially built as a home in the mid-1800's, no doubt belonging to an elite member of society. But now it stood, in its splendid glory, as a solemn reminder of the frailty of life.

As I entered the massive double oak doors, I was greeted with a profound sense of sadness. The air was filled with grief as if a heavy, dark cloud loomed above our heads. I expected nothing less. Making my way through the vast, open room and crowds of people, I searched for a familiar face. In the corner, seated quietly on her own, was Lydia. I immediately went to her side and sat with my hand on hers. Not a word was spoken between us, but sometimes just knowing you're not alone is enough.

After a short while, I broke the silence when I asked Lydia if she had already made her way up to the front of the room to pay her respects. She had not, so together we headed in that direction.

The funeral director had taken much care in creating a warm and inviting atmosphere ... as inviting as it could possibly be under the circumstances. Filled with pastels, champagnes, and ivories, the gentle ambiance of color evoked feelings of comfort. The strategically placed lighting was soft and lent itself to the calming aura the owners had hoped to impart. Photos of Anna dotted the tables in memory of her life once led, while soothing music played softly in the background. From a distance, I couldn't help but notice the plethora of flowers and bouquets that staggered around her casket. And, as we crept our way to the front, her family would come into view. It broke my heart to see her parents so shattered. No mother or father should ever have to experience the loss of a child before themselves. It doesn't matter what age they are. It just isn't right.

Soon enough, there we were, staring down at our once lively and vibrant friend. I had seen so many dead bodies in my career, it was a natural reaction for my brain to start the process of dissecting every small element of the scene. I observed the amethyst-colored rosary she clasped in her hand and noticed the delicate lace details on her dress.

But this scene was different. This was personal. And as I moved around to where her head lay in the casket so that others could pay their respects, I noticed something odd.

It was the lightweight lace, mid-neckline turtleneck that first caught my attention. It seemed out of place with how I remembered Anna's typical choice of attire. First was the delicate lace detail ... Anna was never a fan of more refined choices of clothing. Factor in anything that might cover her neck, especially in the summer, and her style was all wrong. Her typical fashion was all about exposure. She much preferred a more flamboyant and seductive look.

She called it, "The Wow Factor!" At least when we were young, that was her claim to fame. She aimed to personify herself with an element of surprise, wonder, and excitement.

Recognizing her style may be unacceptable for the present occasion, it would seem that those closest to her might select an outfit a bit more representative of her nature ... maybe something Anna would have actually liked to wear.

As I stared at her resting face, a gap in the rim of her neckline caught my eye. The unrestricting edge had created enough of an opening that, through the untrained eye, would appear to cast a shadow upon her neck. But mine were all but untrained, and as I leaned a bit closer, I questioned whether or not the skin under the trim may have actually been discolored. I moved slightly more to the left to get an even closer angle, and of this, I was now sure. The bluish-black pigment staring back at me was, for certain, a discoloration under her skin. Even the makeup didn't fully cover it. But what could it be from? Did she drown as people were saying? And if so, what may have caused the mark? This must have been why they selected the clothing for her that they did.

Edging away from the casket, I found myself face to face with Anna's mother and father.

"What do you say in a situation like this?" I thought to myself.

There are no words … and as I leaned in to hug Anna's mother, my lips parted. The inevitable slipped out, "I'm so sorry for your loss." Then, again, I repeated myself, as I cradled her father in my arms.

It was a heart wrenching moment and I cringe to think I used those words; the most common phrase that people grasp for when there are no other words to be said. It seemed so impersonal, like a robotic response used when we are in an uncomfortable situation. The thought of bearing such an inauthentic and distant message, always bothered me. I can only hope that Anna's parents understood them as my genuine expression of sorrow.

As Lydia and I retreated to a corner in the back of the room, we were soon met by Emily and Jenn. Making small talk amongst each other, my heart skipped a beat and my mind went blank when I saw *him* enter the room. My face went flush in what must have been thirty shades of red. Shock … dismay … excitement … were just a few of the emotions I was feeling. I quickly looked away … I couldn't let him know that I had acknowledged his presence. Isn't that the natural reaction after so many years?

Emily was the first to notice. "Are you ok, Sonya?" she asked.

I had no response and could merely motion with my eyes in the direction he was standing. She looked over as discreetly as she could, and her jaw all but fell off her face.

She said, "Oh my gosh, it's Colin! Colin Griffin!"

By then, Lydia and Jenn had also taken notice of him.

The whispering banter between the three had begun. My head was still swirling, and my thoughts were drowning out every word they said. All I could focus on was the butterflies in my stomach and how well his age was treating him. He still sported that strong, athletic build. He still had that rugged, ruddy look about him. His eyes still glistened that striking pale blue, and his still well-defined jawline accentuated his broad and charming smile. He looked more worldly now … more mature in a masculine way. Instead of sun-streaked hair framing his face, it was lightly peppered with silver streaks, giving him an attractively distinguished look. He modeled a neatly trimmed haircut with day-old stubble that paired well with his high-end and perfectly fitted suit.

"He keeps looking over here, Sonya!" said Jenn.

It is a normal instinct to look in the direction of someone who is looking at you. Especially when someone brings it to your attention. My efforts to ignore him and act as if I hadn't seen him had failed. At the briefest glance, he caught my eye and I labored to turn away. It was only for a moment, but it seemed like an eternity to me. I felt lost in his gaze, even if it was from across the room. He nodded his head, blinked his eyes, and gave me a nonchalant grin. I was so entranced that I doubt I had even gestured back at him. And when the stare was broken, just as quick, he was gone.

Why in the world would all these feelings come rising up to the surface after so many years? I thought I had gotten over him long ago. Or maybe I had simply buried my deepest emotions, along with the painful past that I could never quite outrun. Lost in thought, it was Lydia's words that brought me back to reality.

"You know, Sonya, he never did get married. I think you were the one for him. I'll never understand why you just got up and left the way you did."

I looked at her, searching for words. I had never told anyone why I had left … not my girl clan … not my best friend … not even my own mother.

"I had my reasons," I said. "Just trust me, I had to go."

As we meandered around the room, all four of us were curious to learn more about Anna's death. It appeared, however, that no one really had much to say about it. Occasionally, there would be mention of her drowning and how unfortunate it was. But I really felt that was mere speculation, since she was obviously found on the beach. It just didn't sit right with me. Anna was a talented and well-versed swimmer. The out-of-character way she was dressed for her own funeral, and the discoloration on her neck … of which I could only see a glimpse through the neckline of her ill-selected clothing … lent to my doubt and the gut-wrenching feeling that told me there must be something more.

This thought haunted me throughout the rest of the day and although I was shocked, I can't say I was surprised when I lifted the local newspaper the next morning. I was greeted with the front-page headline that read:

"Local Woman Found Murdered at Gradient Bay"

I literally spit my coffee across the table as my eyes scanned over the words. My poor mother, who was sitting across from me, screeched as she was showered with the spewed hot liquid.

"What in the world?" she exclaimed as she jumped to her feet!

"Oh my gosh, Mom! I am so sorry! But look!" as I turned the newspaper in her direction.

Her mouth dropped open, and for the first time that I could ever remember, she was speechless. As she dusted off her housecoat, I read the article aloud.

"The body of a local woman was found by several beachgoers at Gradient Bay in the city of Duncan, New York in the early morning hours on Saturday, June 22. Duncan Police responded to a call for an unresponsive female where they found Anna Lee Leone, 38. A lifelong Duncan resident, she was last heard from on June 21, on her way to swim at an undisclosed location. Chief of Police Daniel Smathers has confirmed that Anna's death was due to foul play."

I continued, "Anyone with information or who may have seen anything suspicious between the hours of 6:00 p.m. on Friday, June 21 and 6:00 a.m. on Saturday, June 22 are asked to contact the City of Duncan Police Department. All calls will remain anonymous."

As I looked up over the top of the paper, the edges of my mouth arched downward. I read the final somber words: *Justice for Anna!*

I could feel the tears welling up behind my eyes. I can only imagine the sheer terror Anna must have felt, or did she even know she was going to die? What thoughts had gone through her mind during those last moments of her life? What kind of monster would want to take her life?

I turned away from my mother and willed my tears to withdraw. As hard as I tried, a lonely drop slid down my cheek.

CHAPTER 4

The Gift

Sunday, July 7, 2024

I stood solemnly still as the steady pitter-patter of rain beaded down the sides of my umbrella. Ominous-looking clouds hovered above, threatening to choke me in their utterly dark embrace. As the priest said his final "Amen," a spine-tingling gust of wind shook the trees above, sending a fresh deluge of water against my already dampened skin. It was a horribly wet and gloomy morning. It was as though Heaven was angry, and tears were crying down.

Now, trampling across the wet and muddy grass, I breathed a sigh of relief as I was leaving this foreboding place. My first instinct was to forego the luncheon that followed, but instead, I decided to put on my work face and spend the remainder of my afternoon trying to learn as much as I could about Anna's death.

"Ears to the ground" I typically told my staff. I knew this is what I too must do.

Attending Anna's memorial brunch and celebration of life would be the perfect place to do just that. Sometimes less is better; there is a lot you can learn simply by staying silent. Hopefully I might pick up on a detail or two that could prove helpful in the police investigation.

Having my own background in investigations, I also possessed a unique set of skills when it came to criminal profiling. These skills helped me to think outside the box and view things through a nontraditional lens. Like an orthopedist is to a general practitioner, profiling was to investigations. This was *my* expertise. And I was good at it, having spent countless days, weeks, months, and sometimes years developing psychological and behavioral profiles of potential suspects. Even in my sleep, I reviewed, researched, and analyzed … evidence, case files, photos, witness statements, and crime scenes. Many a night I lay awake, afraid to face the demons I'd encountered along the way. I had an unending desire to solve each and every case I was assigned … and even some I wasn't formally assigned. For the few cases I was unable to crack, those would haunt me forever. I could never quite completely let go, always hopeful to one day stumble upon a new lead.

After the article appeared in the *Daily Disturber*, as the local newspaper was more commonly known, people were bound to be buzzing.

So often I would say, "Add a touch of alcohol, and let the truth be told ... secrets unfold." I expected this atmosphere to be no different.

I entered the crowded space. The room was filled with relatives and friends, all too eager to share exaggerated versions of their own personal stories and relationships with the deceased. It is amazing the sheer number of people who come out of the woodwork when someone passes, particularly when it is a high-profile death or an individual of notable character. Both were true in this case. The walls were buzzing with chatter.

As I sauntered around the room and mingled here and there, I picked up some interesting details about Anna's most recent relationship status. There was babble that she had a love interest, but no one knew who it was. There were a couple who even alluded to her having more than one. While Anna was certainly well-loved for all the right reasons, it was abundantly known that she had a wild and racy edge. Combine this with her overly flamboyant nature; she was never one to hide her personal affairs ... particularly when it came to love. So, the question presented itself .... *If she was in a relationship, why was it such a secret?*

I squeezed through the crowded tables and found a seat with Lydia, Emily, and Jenn. I propped myself facing the wall of windows and could see that the rain was subsiding. The sun was trying its hardest to peek out from behind the dimness of the low, hovering clouds.

Maybe it would shine again before the end of the day. For the moment, though, it just felt good to be dry and off my feet.

Setting my elbows on the table and clasping my hands in front of my face, I rested my chin. My mind pondering the rumors, I sat for a moment, and then, louder than I had intended, I blurted out,

"Was Anna seeing someone?"

A few heads at a nearby table briefly turned in my direction, although I had only intended to direct the question to my friends. Instantaneously, all three jumped at the opportunity to respond.

Lydia feverishly shook her head from side to side, from left to right. "No. She hadn't mentioned seeing anyone in at least six months."

Emily chimed in, "She mentioned belonging to a dating site but I talked to her a few days before she died and she still hadn't found any prospects."

Finally, Jenn added, "I really don't think so. She was spending a lot of time training for some kind of athletic competition."

"Six months?" I thought. That was an unusually long time for Anna to be single. I looked at Emily and said, "Do you know what dating app she was using?"

Emily replied, "No, she never mentioned which one, but I know she's been on a ton of them."

Immediately, my mind wandered to the potential that Anna had met someone online … someone she really didn't know … who had other motives than to *just be friends*. I saw a lot of that in my line of work. But why the secretiveness? Could it be he was just a boy toy? Nothing to call home about? Would her parents not approve of whomever her choice was? Even at her age, their opinion mattered. But who knows, maybe there was no lover at all.

With so many questions, I decided I would make one final lap around the room before I gathered my belongings and said my goodbyes. As I slowly made my way through the crowd, I was unexpectedly bumped by an older, somewhat unkempt man. I instantly felt a very uneasy feeling come over me. This chance meeting clearly made me feel uncomfortable, but I just couldn't put my finger on it. I felt like I knew him, but couldn't place where or how.

He was taller than me, with a thin frame. His lanky arms and oversized feet were overshadowed only by his slightly hunched upper body. With stringy, graying hair, his was vagrantly ill-managed and draping recklessly over his shoulders. His unshaven face gave him an appearance of uncleanliness … and those eyes. Those eyes were dark and unnerving. As his gaze met mine, he stared deep into my eyes, as if he could see into the depths of my soul. I knew those eyes; I had seen them before. The gnawing feeling in my gut was one of doom and gloom … a feeling that just wouldn't go away.

After excusing himself, he looked away and, mostly with his head hanging down, he spoke in a monotone voice. "She had a boyfriend, you know."

Lacking emotion and failing to meet my gaze, he proceeded to say, "I know who she was seeing." He had captured my attention as he continued, "You don't need to look very far. He's a married man."

I gasped with eyes wide open and brows raised, waiting for him to continue. There was an awkward, silent pause so I responded, "Well who is it? Who was she seeing?"

The man shook his head as if he was saying "no"; his eyes darted around the room. He was clearly uncomfortable, which was evident in his hasty, nervous movements, scuffling of his feet, and incessant picking at his clothes. In his awkward presence, he refused to divulge the name of Anna's love interest.

"So, what is the purpose of you telling me this?" I asked.

He merely restated, "You don't have to look far." And he swiftly made his escape toward the front door.

I thought about following after him. I believed him, yet I doubted him. My mind was trying to process the validity of his claim. He gave me no lover's name ... no creditable evidence. He failed to provide his identity or how he knew of this supposed affair. The more I thought, the more my doubts were becoming greater than my belief. Although that **would** explain Anna's secretive nature if the rumors were true.

At this point in my thought process, he was gone. Even if I wanted to chase after him, it was too late. But he did make me think. Maybe her death was a crime of passion. Certainly, that is what this mystery man would have me choose to believe.

I found it baffling, however, that I just couldn't shake the formidable feeling I had upon running into him. I hadn't experienced that depth of dreadful emotion since the horrid day that I'd tried so hard to forget ... the day that led me to leave this town in the first place.

As I returned to the table to bid my farewells, Lydia gazed at me. With eyes narrowed and a visible frown in her brow, she said, "Who was that man?"

I curiously looked at her and tilted my head in question. Lydia said, "He looked so out of place here."

I explained to Lydia that it felt as if I knew him, and told her how I had felt standing in his presence.

She continued, "He's not a townie. I can't say I've ever seen him before and I can't imagine what his association with Anna may have been."

I thought to myself, "It can't be a coincidence that he bumped into me. Clearly, he knew what he was doing."

Most of the time, people are intimidated by who I am and what I represent in my line of work. He was not. I guess there is always the possibility that he didn't know who I was or what I did, "So why me then? In a room full of all those people, why me?" I mumbled out loud.

While he displayed some signs of discomfort, his ability to stare deep into my eyes showed confidence. It seemed evident that he had a reason for garnering my attention. Recognizing that he could just be a whacko hanging around for a free meal, I didn't want to completely dismiss him. You just never know, he could prove to be something more than a chance meeting. I would definitely make a mental note of this *mystery man*.

As odd as it may seem, what stood out the most about him was how he made me feel. Ever since I can remember, I have had a very intrinsic sense of intuition … a sixth sense some might say … or third eye. There are some that might rationalize their inner voices with science; I prefer to think of those voices as my *Angel* … an angel guiding me in the right direction, keeping me out of harm's way. I believe that everyone has one. Whether we listen to it or not is purely a personal choice.

35

I learned a long time ago to listen to mine. It was actually at a time that I didn't listen to it, that I learned the value it served. Call me crazy; I call it both a gift and a blessing. It's like a warning system harbored in my subconscious. It warns me of troubling situations and nefarious encounters. It is like a bridge, gapping the space between my subconscious and my conscious minds.

This particular encounter was strong. I could feel it in my gut and right to my core. Back in the day, Lydia would tease me and brush off my feelings. She was always the skeptical one. And I must admit that back then, I was a bit skeptical too.

What I learned along the way, though, is that sometimes people prefer to discount what they just don't understand. For them, it's easier that way. But it's true that everyone has a gut instinct or inner voice. While some voices scream, others only whisper ... while some people listen, others choose to ignore.

In the case of this mystery man, a logical person might say it was his outward appearance that made me feel the way I felt. I say, however, that it is the illogical mind that recognizes that intuition goes far deeper than pure logic. This man's ominous aura convinced me that there was something far more sinister about him. And somehow, I knew those piercing eyes; I had met them before.

CHAPTER 5

No Stone Unturned

Monday, July 8, 2024

As I prepared my bags for my departing flight the next morning, my phone rang. I recognized the number to be that of Michael James, my work colleague and personal confidante back in Virginia.

He usually didn't call my personal cell phone, so "it must be something important," I thought to myself.

When I answered his call, Michael greeted me with his usual, "Hey, Lady. How are things going?"

It was unlike Michael to beat around the bush. Before I could even respond, he got right to the point. "Remember the case file we looked over a few years ago? The one where the girl went missing from a small town in Ohio … they found her near the edge of the water on Lake Erie with a red ribbon tied around her neck."

"You mean the one that had absolutely no leads? I sure do!" I responded.

He proceeded, "Well, there is a similar scenario about an hour away from your hometown there in New York. Law enforcement in Pennsylvania has requested assistance from us. There is chatter about some similarities with the Ohio case. Your boss, Cristo, was going to send someone from that region. I recommended he send you instead, since you are right there, of course."

He chuckled as he continued, "Besides, you're the best!"

That was Michael, always looking out for me. He knew how I had missed not having enough time with my mother and thought this would be a chance for me to remain in my hometown a little longer. What he didn't know was the details about Anna's death. It was with a heavy heart that I would be leaving and not be able to do anything to assist in bringing her perpetrator to justice. Some extra time might allow me to do a little of my own investigation into her untimely passing. I jumped at the opportunity to extend my stay and thanked him profusely for thinking of me.

Michael indicated that the Pennsylvania murder took place about two months ago. He spoke of the similarities between the several-year-old Ohio case and this one. Both involved victims who were young, college-aged girls in their early twenties, of petite build, and with long dark hair. Both were avid swimmers and athletically inclined. Both were sexually assaulted. Both strangled victims were found on a Lake Erie beach, in small remote areas, with a single red ribbon tied around their necks.

"Wow," I thought to myself. "Sounds like the work of the same person."

I learned early on in my job, though, never to assume the obvious. Being the skeptic that I am, I'll never accept one particular scenario just because it seems like the most palpable choice. In this case, the Ohio murder took place three years earlier. Having had heavy media coverage, it wouldn't take much for someone to copycat the details of that case. To assume both were connected, without giving each case proper consideration, would be an injustice to the victims.

I looked down at my watch. It was only 10:02 a.m. I could take a quick trip to Pennsylvania, make formal introductions, and peruse the details of the case.

"Can you send me the Ohio case file?" I asked Michael.

"Consider it done, Sonny," he replied.

A subtle curve of my lips acknowledged his use of the nickname that only my closest friends were accustomed to. I was so happy to have Michael as one of them.

I arrived at the Ackerton Police Department at about 11:30 a.m. I could tell when I entered the station that it was a rather small unit. Housed in a historic building in the center of town, this was not the bustling community I was accustomed to working in, but rather, a small, impoverished town in the middle of nowhere. I was convinced that if it hadn't been for its location on the water's edge, it would be easily missed on the map.

Following introductions, I was led to a private room. "This will be your workspace."

The officer continued, "Chief Smith was expecting someone from your agency but not quite this soon. In any case, he will be here a little later today. I will let him know that you are here. Until then, make yourself at home. If you need anything at all, I'm here to assist you. My name is Officer Donnelly."

I shook the young officer's cold, clammy hand. He appeared to be a bit nervous, but overall, a fine and well-spoken officer of the law.

"Thank you," I replied as I turned around and faced a litany of photos sprawled across the desk.

"The most difficult part," I thought to myself. "This was always the most difficult part ... having to dissect the visuals of a case."

As I glanced around at the items in the room, one particular photo caught my eye. There she was ... young female, about age twenty-two … fair-skinned with long, dark hair. Her wavy locks softly framed her delicate, feminine features. She was quite attractive as she lay limp and naked on her back, with the water's edge touching her toes … eyes gently closed. She almost looked peaceful. She obviously took great care with her physical appearance, and for what? For it to end like this? The perpetrator also seemed to have taken a great amount of care of the victim. I would suggest that the body was positioned in such a way as to take the lake tides into consideration; any miscalculation and she could have been swept away in the unruly waves that frequented this body of water. Or maybe that was the intent, and a miscalculation had been made. Another thought to add to my litany of inquiries.

I sat down before the photos, noticing that this one was quite dimly lit. I presumed it was shot in the early morning hours, just as the sun was rising. The darkness of the sky seamlessly met the murkiness of the water. Even the hard, gray slate she laid sprawled on took on a solemn coldness atypical for the time of year she was killed. A depressing and mortifying backdrop surrounded her; it screamed of somber affliction … all except for the single red ribbon, tied in a nice, neat bow around her neck. My heart sank, as it usually did in a situation such as this. I remember that red bow well. Our girl in Ohio had the same thing tied around her neck.

The first question that came to mind was, "What hand was that bow tied with?"

As I had recalled from Ohio, the perpetrator was identified as being left-handed. Zooming in on a variety of photos on a magnifier, I carefully followed the direction of the ribbon. I could tell that this, too, had been tied by a left-handed person. It wasn't much to go on, but it did potentially eliminate about 90% of the population as suspects. This, of course, assumed that the perp used his or her dominant hand to tie the bow and did not purposely use their other hand in an effort to throw off the investigation. It also assumed that the perp was not ambidextrous, which would have meant he was able to use both hands with equal ease. Those who are ambidextrous only account for a very small percentage of the population, however. At only 1%, it would still eliminate the majority of the population of suspects when added to the number of lefties who could have potentially tied it.

Pushing the photos aside, I found a large notepad on the table with almost illegible writing on it. Raising it closer to my eyes in an attempt to decipher the henpecked print, it appeared to read:

Signs of sexual encounter
Forensics detected no sperm – No DNA
No signs of struggle
No evidence that the body had been moved
Cause of death: strangulation – fractured hyoid bone
Time of death: 5/23/2024 8:30 pm – 5/24/24 3:30 am

A million more questions started rolling through my mind. "Did she know her attacker? Was it a Lover? Could it be the same lover as our Ohio gal? Or, is this just a coincidence? Maybe a copycat? Could she have been lured to this remote location? If so, how?" The list goes on and on.

I've always had a difficult time with the "why's" of a case. What could possibly motivate a human being to take the life of another? With so many questions already, I knew there would be many more. Through my contemplation, I closed my eyes, rested my forehead in my hands, and envisioned what might have possibly transpired during her last moments of life.

My thoughts were suddenly interrupted by a slight tapping on the door. As my focus was broken, I looked up over my hands. I gazed in complete and utter disbelief, my lower jaw gaping toward the floor. Two gentlemen were standing in the doorway … one in particular had captured my attention.

I stood up from where I had been seated, suddenly frozen in time. I was barely able to move and nearly unable to speak. Every thought I previously had in my mind went blank. It was Colin! Colin Griffin! And by the expression on his face, he was just as flabbergasted to see me too. Of course, he would have had no idea I would be standing there. Even if he had been privy to my name before entering the room, I no longer carried my maiden name, of which he would have been familiar. Our expressions literally mirrored one another.

It was an awkward few moments, though it seemed like much longer, when the other gentleman finally spoke. He obviously observed the incredulous look upon our faces. "You know each other?"

As Colin and I stumbled upon words, he introduced himself as Chief Jeremy Smith from the Ackerton Police Department. He proceeded, "And this is Officer Colin Griffin, lead investigator for the Duncan Police Department in New York. Am I correct to assume that you two already know each other?"

As my senses returned to me, I extended my hand to Chief Smith and then to Officer Griffin and introduced myself, "Sonya Morrison, Criminal Profiler with the FBI Serial Investigations Unit in Virginia. Nice to meet you."

Neither Colin nor I entertained a response to Chief Smith's reference to our being acquainted.

Chief Smith, or Chief Jeremy, as he was more famously known, was a late middle-aged man in his mid-fifties. He was tall and slim with the exception of a slight belly that peaked out over his belt line. His clean-shaven appearance highlighted his moss green eyes that stood out under his wildly tousled brown hair. There was an almost wholesome, yet mysterious, presence about him. I was glad he didn't pay much attention to mine and Colin's awkwardness. Instead of lingering on how we knew each other, he proceeded right with the case.

Chief Jeremy acknowledged that I had already been reviewing some of the information in the room. He indicated that there was a possible connection between this girl and a three-year-old case from Ohio that remained unsolved. Of course, I was already familiar with the Ohio case. It was the case I had reviewed; we were unable to add to the local investigation because the killer left an immaculate crime scene. If there *is* such a thing as an immaculate crime scene, that was it.

What I didn't know was what he was about to say next. Chief Jeremy went on to explain that a similar case in Chattacoin County, New York, also involved similar attributes. My interest piqued as I raised my brows.

He added, "Including a red ribbon tied around the victim's neck."

He continued to explain that while there may be some inconsistencies, they weren't going to rule out any possibilities. My thoughts swirled since I wasn't aware of another case involving a red ribbon, especially one that took place in my home county.

"What in the world had happened to the area I grew up in? How many murders had there been since I left?" I thought to myself.

I asked, "Really? Have you identified the victim in Chattacoin County?"

Colin responded in a solemn voice, "It's Anna, Sonny."

"What?" I exclaimed! "No way! Not my friend, Anna!" I could feel my limbs begin to tremble as I considered a possible connection between *my* Anna and the young woman I observed in the photos. "You really think there might be a connection?" I asked.

Both men nodded simultaneously, without saying a word.

Chief Jeremy broke the silence with, "That is where you come in. The red ribbon might seem to be a dead giveaway, but we need more. While each case shared similarities and their relatedness would seem obvious, we need to be sure."

I clearly recalled that the red ribbon was one of several features leaked by the media when the Ohio gal was found. I wasn't going to give up on the theory that someone could pull up an old newspaper and easily copycat similar details.

Chief Jeremy continued, "We need to either confirm the connection or eliminate the possibility. There are too many commonalities to simply dismiss; yet, we can't assume and get it wrong."

My nod of agreement was followed by Chief Jeremy's voice. "You'll be working closely with Officer Griffin and me during this investigation. Normally, I would never consider involving someone on the investigative team who has such close ties with, in this case, one of the victims. But your reputation precedes you. And you are already familiar with the case in Ohio. Can I assume that this will not be a problem?"

As I stumbled on my initial words, I finally spewed, "Not a problem at all."

I wasn't quite sure if he was referring to my association with Anna or the unspoken connection with Colin. Maybe he meant both. In any case, my professional cap was on! I would approach this assignment with the same analytical mindset, dedication, and professionalism that I would approach any other case. I'd remain true to my motto, *Leave No Stone Unturned*. My end goal was always to do my very best to give each of these victims and their families the personal, most respectful, and totally unbiased attention toward the closure they deserved.

Meanwhile, the butterflies in my belly had returned, and in the back of my mind, a little voice said, "Did he REALLY just call you Sonny?"

CHAPTER 6

Who Is Fred?

Monday, July 8, 2024

Before leaving Ackerton, I decided to take a ride to the crime scene. From the public parking area, I followed a sandy path that meandered through wispy blades of tall American beachgrass. A somewhat secluded area, huge sheets of slate were scattered throughout this cobble, sand, and pebble shore. As I approached the area, I observed the remnants of crime scene tape still lingering in the breeze. This was where the Pennsylvania victim breathed her last breath, here upon these slabs of cold, gray stone. Recalling years back to the Ohio case, it was uncanny how eerily similar the two locations were.

I walked around the area, viewing it from different angles. I tried to put myself in the victim's shoes, imagining what she was thinking. I glanced out to the east and could see a couple of people off in the distance. This was obviously not a popular spot and had proven to be the perfect secluded location for our perp.

I walked over to the area where the victim's car had been parked. I wanted to see for myself why law enforcement had such a difficult time retrieving tire and footprints. They had said the weather on the evening of her death brought heavy winds and that the area consisted of mostly sand. Visiting the area quickly confirmed how easily this vast, open area could succumb to the forces of nature.

It had been a long day, so I decided to take the scenic route home along Lake Erie Road. Lake Erie Road was a long, winding stretch between Ackerton and Duncan that followed the length of the lake's edge. It was a nice, refreshing seventy-two-degree drive, and as I looked at the clock on my dash, I saw that it was already 8:56 p.m. The sun was setting, and the sky was aglow. And Wow! What a beautiful and glorious sight to see! There was absolutely nothing like a Western New York sunset over Lake Erie; I had forgotten how magnificent it was.

As I drove along, trailing behind me were intermingling shades of yellow, peach, orange, and red. The colors were vibrantly and seamlessly blending into one another, creating unique hues of varying depth. At the core was a brilliant orange half circle that appeared to be effortlessly melting into an endless sea. Each of the colors bounced off the glass-like, glistening water, like a mirror reflecting the abstract beauty from above. The view and colors were so spectacular, it was as if I was looking at a vividly painted postcard that was just out of my reach.

My mind wandered ... first to Anna, then to the PA victim, and finally to the Ohio girl. All found by these breathtaking waters. How could something so beautiful harbor such horrific secrets? Evidence would suggest that each of these ladies may have, in fact, experienced their final sunset, exactly as it appeared tonight, shortly before they died.

Lost in thought, I was halfway through the drive when my phone rang. Looking at the screen, I saw Emily's name light up. I thought to myself that it was a bit late for a social call, unless of course she was drunk. How I hated trying to converse with a drunk. I hesitated to answer her call and waved my finger over the screen with the thought of ending it altogether. But, in my hesitation, I accidentally tapped the answer button. Cringing at my error, I could hear Emily on the other end incessantly calling my name.

"Sonny, are you there? Sonny?"

She sounded frantic, so I responded, "Hey Emily, what's up?"

Like water gushing out of a spigot, Emily began ranting in a desperate tone. I could barely understand what she was saying, but I did catch "arrested ... Fred ... affair ... Anna."

I interrupted as pleasantly as I could, trying to calm her down so I could hear what she was saying. Her tear-filled voice explained that her husband had been locked in jail under the suspicion of Anna's murder. She said that it had come to light that he had been involved in a six-month affair with Anna, right under her nose. She had no idea and was completely blindsided. The police had alluded to this being a crime of passion.

"Of passion?!" I exclaimed. "Wait, slow down. Start from the beginning."

She took a couple of deep breaths. Still in a whimper, Emily explained that she and Fred, her husband, had been sitting in the kitchen around 11:00 a.m. While chatting over a late breakfast, the local county sheriff showed up at their door. He had begun, almost instantly, with a barrage of questions. He was quizzing Fred with questions from the extent of Fred's relationship with Anna to where he was on the night of her murder. They asked him to come to the station so he could make a formal statement. They alluded to that it was just a formality. Not thinking much of it, Fred complied with the officer. She explained that while on their way there, she wanted Fred to contact an attorney, but he insisted he was innocent and felt this visit would be of no consequence.

Emily continued to tell how she was in a state of shock the whole time and that she really couldn't remember half of what any of the officers said to her. Of course, she was not allowed to be present when they questioned Fred at the station, but she was steadfast in saying that he obstinately denied any kind of romantic relationship with Anna. After hours upon hours of waiting, it was early evening when Emily watched two officers walk Fred out of the interrogation room, hands cuffed behind his back, and led him down a hallway and through another door ... not to be seen again.

"I just don't know what to do. I need your help!" Emily said.

What a conundrum I was in. On one hand, I have Fred, who is arrested by the county for Anna's murder; at the same time, I am looking at Anna's death being connected to two other murders. On the other hand, I have Fred's wife asking me to help her because he has been arrested. All I could do in the moment was try to put Emily's mind at ease.

I explained that while the Sheriff may believe they have established motive, if Fred was truly innocent, they would have nothing more to support their case. I further explained that if Fred really had no romantic involvement with Anna, then they wouldn't even have a motive. I told Emily that I would stop in at the Sheriff's Office first thing in the morning and see what I could learn. Until then, I reassured her that he would be safe while in custody in a small, albeit uncomfortable, holding cell. Though it is rarely anyone's desire to spend the night in jail, at least he was at a small-town county facility where the violent criminal population was limited in comparison to some of the larger facilities. Hopefully, they have not formally charged him and will have insufficient evidence to do so. Then, they will have to release him. In any case, I directed her to contact an attorney with expertise in criminal defense ... preferably, someone who is known in the area for their honorable and respectable reputation ... someone with experience and who has handled the defense of other violent offender cases.

"He will be safe! Don't worry," I assured her.

With that said and done, I wondered what the county involvement was with Anna's case. There seemed to be a disconnect between the local Duncan station and them. Otherwise, Colin would surely have mentioned the forthcoming arrest.

I pondered on my meeting with Chief Jeremy and Colin. Chief Jeremy had indicated that he was in the preliminary stages of establishing an investigative team; depending on the outcome of some of the analysis he had requested from me, it would determine the direction they take. He also pointed out Colin's popular and impressive reputation within the region for handling violent crime-related investigations. That, and the fact that Anna's murder occurred within his area of jurisdiction, made Colin's presence today completely logical.

At this point, our mission was highly confidential; very few entities were aware that we were considering a multi-murder scenario. The County Sheriff's Office may not have had much knowledge of the murder in PA. Working within their county, they were likely under the presumption that Anna's death was one of a single, isolated crime. Still, why hadn't Colin been aware of the impending arrest? Or maybe he was. Why, then, wouldn't he mention it to me?

As I drove the rest of the way home, I wondered about Fred. Who was he really? I didn't have much of an opportunity to get to know him personally. I had already moved away from Duncan when he and Emily were dating and got married. They came to visit me once, early in their relationship. But beyond that visit, I only knew what Emily had shared over the years in the telephone conversations we had. None of which was very impressive.

She described him as her knight in shining armor in the beginning. They had fallen quickly and madly in love and wasted no time with getting married and starting a family. He was, at the time, a hard worker and believed in traditional family values. His view was that the woman stays at home, cooks the meals, does the laundry, and takes care of the kids. Emily knew this early on and was content with the idea. But then, as the years passed, Fred began drinking more. What started out as weekly social outings with friends, turned into part of his daily routine. With his drinking, he had become more condescending and abusive toward her. They say you tend to hurt those you are closest to; nothing could be truer in their case.

According to Emily, Fred had made a name for himself over the years. While he was typically the life of the party, he had become known for his intermittent explosive outbursts. Typically, these outbursts resulted in angry verbal attacks or temper tantrums that involved throwing or breaking objects. There were even instances of his aggressive behavior having resulted in his being thrown out of several local bars. In most cases, his reactions seemed far more extreme than the given situation. It all culminated when he was involved in a road rage incident that resulted in his arrest. I wasn't ever privy to what had come out of that matter, but it seemed to me that it only made him more reclusive, bored, and angry. I tried to impress on Emily, a few years back, that he showed symptoms of a condition called Intermittent Explosive Disorder. I urged her to seek him the help he needed. Whether he accepted it or not, I pled for her to seek help for herself … for her own self-preservation, so she might gain a better understanding of the situation and learn strategies to help them both. It fell on deaf ears. And, this is where it brought us.

Could he be guilty of what he was accused of? I definitely thought he could be! On the other hand, could there be a biased opinion among local law enforcement based on his previous record of behavior? Absolutely! Of this, I was sure.

Even though theirs had not been the happily ever after Emily dreamed of, she refused to leave his side. She adamantly professed that they still had many more happy times than bad, and that is what she clung onto. She still believed in her own little fairytale and was convinced that one day, the knight she met a long time ago would come back to her. As tactfully as I tried through the years, there was no getting her to realize the reality of her situation. So, I had eventually given up. Sure, I would always be there if she needed me, but sometimes you have to distance yourself from a situation when it causes you an unresolvable level of stress or anxiety, particularly when the person you are trying to help has no desire to change the situation from its current form. As difficult as it was, I had to accept that you can't help those who won't help themselves. That's the point I had reached with Emily.

But what about his formative years? What was he like growing up? Could he be capable of a more diabolical and calculated plan? More than just an isolated killing out of deep passion?

From what I recall, Fred had a normal childhood upbringing. He came from a close-knit family and grew up on a small farm in a rural community not much different than ours. Nothing that Emily ever shared stood out to indicate he was capable of what he had been accused of, at least not from a serial perspective should Anna's death be connected to the Ohio and Pennsylvania cases. But in a crime of passion, I most definitely believed he was capable. In this situation, the perpetrator doesn't typically plan their attack; it is not a premeditated act of aggression. And since there has been no well-thought-out process, it is typically the result of an impulsive act committed in the *heat of passion*. Fred's past behavior had set him up perfectly for this scenario. I knew it, and local law enforcement knew it. That is, if Fred was, in fact, having an affair with Anna. THAT was the multi-million-dollar question!

Now, I had two very different scenarios to consider.

Was Anna's death a crime of passion?

Or, was there a serial killer in our backyard?

The red ribbon would seem to be a dead giveaway—a sure connection to the latter. But then again, there might also be a third scenario to ponder. Maybe … quite possibly …

… BOTH of these scenarios were true.

CHAPTER 7

Fork In The Road

Tuesday, July 9, 2024

I hadn't gotten much sleep. Probably a culmination of the previous days' unsettling events. First was the realization that Anna's murder may be connected with two others. Next was finding out I will be working with Colin while I'm looking at this case. Then, I learned that Emily's husband may have been having an affair with Anna. And finally, there was Fred's arrest for potentially murdering Anna. Oh, the tangled webs we weave.

As I sat at the kitchen table sipping coffee with my mother, I asked her what she knew about Fred. She inquisitively stared back at me as she set her cup down on the table.

"Emily's Fred?" she asked.

"Yes. Emily's Fred," I responded.

"Not a bad guy, I suppose. I know he's had his issues. *They've* had their issues. But he's a good dad." She responded. "Why do you ask?"

I knew that the local newspaper, *The Daily Disturber*, would be jumping on the opportunity to print something about Fred's arrest. It hadn't appeared as of this morning, or Mom would have brought it up first. This particular news outlet was quite notorious for printing whatever they thought might grab the reader's attention. It didn't matter how shocking the news was or who they hurt. Sometimes it didn't even matter that only half-truths were being told. This story would receive no mercy, so I knew it was coming soon.

There was no doubt in my mind that word would travel even quicker than the press in this small community. With this in mind, I had hoped to get a hometown perspective of what Fred's potential involvement could've been. I have found that, oftentimes, the local townies know more than local law enforcement does. My mother was no exception. She was a haven of knowledge when it came to hometown happenings, and she had a keen intuition about the people in general. Since no rumors had started yet, I had hoped to enlist my mother's unbiased opinion. There was no one I trusted more than my own mother.

I shared with Mom that Fred was in jail as well as some of Emily's basic details. She was both shocked and horrified. Fervently shaking her head back and forth as if indicating a negative response, she said, "I will never believe it! Affair, maybe ... Murder, never! Not under any circumstance!"

I wasn't really expecting that response. She was so sure of herself. I asked her how she could be so confident in her assertion. She went on to explain that although Fred was not from Duncan, she knew his family quite well. They were from the next county over, and she even knew Fred when he was younger. She said that while he may have his faults, as we all do, sometimes you just know what people are or are not capable of. The person he is when he is sober made him a joy to be around. She qualified herself by saying that she actually only knows him as being sober but that she's heard some of the nasty rumors. Her experience with him was that of a funny, kind, and charismatic man.

"And he really is a great father. I don't believe he is capable of such a horrific act. Not by a long shot!" she said.

Mom proceeded to explain how his heavier drinking came about. He had worked in a local factory for most of his life, and when they suddenly shut down, he lost his livelihood. He went into work one morning, only to be greeted with a padlock on the door. It was like a piece of him was lost with the company that day. He had invested all his time and energy into that place. He had all his stocks in there too, and they just went belly up. He lost everything. Days turned into weeks, which turned into months, and then years. She talked about depression being a nasty burden to carry.

"It changes people, but it doesn't change their heart. Not deep down it doesn't," she said.

"I don't know what happened between him and Emily, but his kids are what's kept him alive all these years. He would never hurt his children like this."

Before ending the conversation, Mom threw in a last tidbit of information. She had questioned who had arrested Fred. Upon realizing it was Sheriff Howard, she stated, "You know, there is history between Sheriff Howard and Fred. Back in the day, they were both dating Emily and vying for her attention. Emily ultimately chose Fred, and Sheriff Howard took it pretty hard. It is said that he still carries a torch for her, and he hasn't liked Fred ever since."

That certainly gave me some food for thought. Knowing about Fred and Sheriff Howard's past led me to believe that what had just happened to Fred may have been influenced in some way, realized or not, by a personal vendetta. I took it with a grain of salt though, as I did her overall opinion of Fred, being fully aware that you never really know what goes on in someone's mind. Even still, I was glad we had that conversation because it gave me a more compassionate view of the man he might have been under different circumstances. I actually had a moment of enlightenment as to why Emily had insisted on staying with him for so long … hopelessly awaiting the return of the love she once knew. Their relationship was so incredibly sad, yet probably so very common in our current society.

I arrived at the Sheriff's Office just before 10:00 a.m. I introduced myself and requested to speak with Sheriff Howard. In no time at all, I was shuffled into a quaint, little office. It was nothing fancy, but it comfortably housed a large wooden desk with a faux leather, high-back chair seated behind it. There was additional seating for three and a couple of very unique, unusually antiquated, wooden filing cabinets along the back wall. The room's easterly-facing window allowed just enough sunlight to brighten the room without requiring overhead illumination. The walls were lined with countless awards and decorations. It was actually quite impressive.

As I was admiring the wall décor, the sound of a male clearing his throat came from behind me. Startled, I quickly spun around in his direction. It was Colin … again!

"I see you've beaten me here," he said.

I'm quite sure I was gaping again, mouth wide open, jaw to the floor, and maybe even a little starstruck. He just keeps popping up in the most unexpected places. Although the sight of him both shocked and excited me, I was a little more at ease than I was the previous day; I must be getting used to these surprise encounters.

He explained that he had learned of Fred's detainment late last night when he had returned home. Although he wanted to tell me first thing this morning, he thought he would get as many details as he could before presenting the news to me. That was just like the Colin I remembered, always very detailed and calculated in his thinking. But I already knew, and here we were, thinking the same way. We had come up with the same plan to show up here at the Sheriff's Office at the same time. The thought was a bit scary.

I chuckled to myself as I thought, "Great minds think alike."

Being a local law enforcement officer, I'm sure he knew that he was better positioned to gather privy information. I knew this too, so when he suggested we talk with the sheriff together, I was in full agreement. Then, in walked Sheriff Howard.

With all introductions complete, Sheriff Howard shut the door, and we all sat down to discuss the matter of *Fred*. It sounded like all they had at this point were accusations from two supposedly *very reliable sources* that Fred and Anna were involved in an intimate relationship. Thus far, Fred had denied the affair and had an alibi. He had a rock-solid alibi. As Sheriff Howard spoke about Fred, I noted a condescending tone; it was obvious he had zero respect and certainly no love lost for the man. He let out a snide grin when he spoke about some of the more recent findings of Anna's autopsy that showed there were sperm in her ovaries. As I was well aware, this could happen if she had sex within seven days of the autopsy. While that may not place Fred at the immediate murder scene, it certainly would discredit his honesty about an intimate affair.

I looked at Colin, and he looked at me with the same astonished expression. Apparently, he was not yet aware of this particular finding. I could tell he was caught off guard that Sheriff Howard had this information before him.

"We are currently awaiting results on a match with Mr. Fred Jones," said Sheriff Howard.

Again, I looked at Colin. The look on his face was a dead giveaway that he was even less aware that they were actively testing Fred's DNA. I knew, all too well, the feeling you get when it seems like someone is stepping on your toes. It must have taken Colin every ounce of restraint not to lash out at Sheriff Howard.

I stood there, secretly hoping there was no match. Partly because of Sheriff Howard's arrogant attitude, but mostly for Emily's sake. Knowing what I knew about Fred, though, my gut was telling me otherwise. Colin and I continued to stand in silence. Neither of us was allowed to divulge any information on the connection we were working on between Anna and the two other murder victims.

Sheriff Howard got up from behind his desk, placed both hands on his hips, spread his legs apart, and looked at me with an inquisitive look. He questioned, "And why is someone of your stature and expertise interested in a small hometown case like this?"

He caught me off guard, but I was quick on my toes with my response. I showed no remarkable reaction to his inquiry. I explained that I happened to be in town and said, "I am long-time friends with both the deceased and the suspect's wife. Naturally, I'm interested in this case. Since I'm in the area, I thought I'd offer my assistance, if needed."

He was appreciative of my offer, and my response seemed to satisfy his curiosity when Colin rebutted. Colin rose up from his chair and assumed a similar stance when he said, "And why is the county stepping on the city's toes with this one? You went out and took a suspect into custody for a case that is in MY jurisdiction, without even the courtesy of a word."

I thought to myself, "Oh boy. Here we go."

Colin had done so well holding back until now. He definitely had a legitimate concern, but was this a defensive reaction to the Sheriff's questioning of me that broke the camel's back? It sure seemed like it by the tone in Colin's voice, the way he stood, and how he framed his question.

One could feel the friction building in the room. After a bit of back and forth, it all boiled down to an obscure boundary line, which was expected to be resolved later in the day. While they were both free to work on the case together, "together" was the key word. A final determination regarding who would take the lead, however, would be made based on the locality of the deceased body and where that boundary line occurred. Of course, that was all dependent on whether or not Anna's death was associated with the Pennsylvania and Ohio cases. If it was, then it became a federal matter.

As I stood to leave, there arose a commotion in the lobby. It was Fred's attorney who was raising all kinds of noise. He had come to pick up Fred. Apparently, there had been no formal arrest, and he came to demand his client's release. Sheriff Howard flew from his chair to join in on the noise.

He scurried out of the office, and looking over his shoulder at us, his last words were, "We'll see him back here tomorrow when those results come back with a match."

I thought to myself, "Not if this case goes in the direction I think it may go or if the city ends up with jurisdiction."

I looked at Colin and said, "We really need to talk to Fred."

He nodded in agreement.

"I know it looks bad if he lied about an affair, but even if he did, he is still only guilty of adultery. They said he has a rock-solid alibi. They are going to have to get more than a matching week-old sperm to bring him in again."

I was almost feeling sorry for Fred. Was he in this situation because he was guilty by association? After talking with my mother this morning, it sure seemed like that was a viable possibility.

I followed Colin back to the Duncan Police Department. My plan for the day was to review the evidence and information they had so I could formulate a preliminary picture of what had happened to Anna. I had hoped with this information, I might be able to make a connection to the Pennsylvania and Ohio cases. While Duncan and Ackerton law enforcement had their own opinions, a lot of weight was on my shoulders to confirm or deny their suspicions. If it turned out there was, indeed, a connection between two or all three, this matter would elevate to a whole new level.

Right away and to get me started, I reviewed analysis and forensic results, crime scene photos, samples that were taken from the site, and witness statements. While looking through the photos, a critical question that comes to mind is, "Who is in the background?"

Often times, the perpetrator will return to the crime scene and it is not unlike them to return when the investigators are there. To them, it's a crude form of taunting used to stroke their own disillusioned and deluded minds. While there were bystanders in some of the photos, no one really stood out. It would be important to compare these photos to those of the other murder scenes to see if they contained a common element.

Tomorrow I was expecting to receive the documents I'd requested on the Ohio case. While many of the details were still ingrained in my mind, I wanted to leave no room for error. I could compare my notes and observations I made yesterday in Ackerton, along with those previously made in Ohio, to those I developed today on Anna. I hoped that by the end of the week, I might be able to provide the confirmation or declination Chief Jeremy was looking for.

My feelings were mixed on the direction I was hoping this case would take. I was enjoying the time spent with my mom and generally, just being here in Duncan. It was also a satisfying feeling that I could be influential in solving a case that was near and dear to my heart. On the other hand, if there was no connection, I could return to Virginia and be with my children. "Oh, how I was missing them," I thought.

It appeared I had reached a fork in the road. Not knowing which path I would follow, the next couple of days would determine my final direction.

CHAPTER 8

A New Direction

Sunday, July 14, 2024

I woke up feeling accomplished. After receiving the Ohio case files on Wednesday, I had decided I would become a total recluse while I reviewed all three cases. So, on Thursday, I had settled into a little cottage along the shore of Lake Erie, setting the tone for what I knew would be a long, grueling weekend. I wanted no interruptions ... no distractions.

It was a quaint and cozy little place that I found last minute through an online rental agency. The décor was fresh and clean with a coastal vibe. It was set in off-white and various hues of seafoam green. Pretty coral-colored accents added just the right pop of color.

The living area is where I set up shop. With a grand, whitewashed coffee table set in the center of the room, it allowed for a massive work area where I could easily lay out the documents and notes I needed to review. The open concept design allowed additional workspace on the twelve-person dining table a few steps away. The northern length of the room faced the water, which was easily visible through the glass wall that sat before me. I would spend many pausing moments staring out those windows, thinking about the victims, imagining what their last moments must have been like.

When I needed a break to clear my mind, I found a bit of solitude walking out the patio door onto the expansive sandy beach. Under my toes, the tiny granules were soft and warmed by the rays of the sun. Slowly, I'd make my way toward the water, fully entertained by the beautifully colored rocks and occasional piece of beach glass peeking through the sand. I would imagine their journey tossing seamlessly through the waves for years or even decades before they found their resting place on shore. So perfectly tumbled, each had a story as unique as its beauty. To me, they represented a metaphor for people who get lost in the waves of life, only to find themselves again, more beautiful than before.

Who was I kidding? *They* were, in fact, representative of *me*. Only, I was still adrift, tumbling in the waves. Until I could heal that part of me that died twenty years ago, would I then become that pretty little treasure that washes up on shore?

Sitting at the edge of the clear, calm water, I'd observe an occasional rolling wave. Like music to my ears, the wandering seagulls sang in synch with the wallowing tides. This picturesque setting was only occasionally disrupted by a goose or two floating by. Even they, in their glory, added to the serenity of it all. Sitting out in this vast space with no one else in sight was like a breath of fresh air. Here I was able to experience a sense of peace and tranquility I hadn't felt in a long time. Though I longed to stay on this beach endlessly, fifteen minutes at a time was enough to recharge and refocus my senses back to the reason I was there in the first place.

Through three arduous days and three sleepless nights, I scoured the information I had at my disposal. I reviewed interviews, notes, and forensic data and reports. I looked for patterns and commonalities between the cases. Filling in the gaps or looking to answer lingering questions, I referred to the information-sharing software and databases I had access to. By analyzing the crime patterns and offender behavior, I worked on developing criminal and victim profiles as well as geographical trends. I studied each victim in an attempt to understand the offender's motivation for selection. The patterns and consistencies were irrefutable.

Even though there was still so much to do, I settled on my recommendation, of which I was highly confident. I was eager to share my findings with Chief Jeremy, so although it was Sunday, I rang the police station to see if he was in. "Ackerton Police Department." I heard a familiar voice say on the other end of the line.

It was Chief Jeremy. He welcomed my visit, so instead of heading directly home, I steered myself in the opposite direction, heading west, toward Pennsylvania.

Once I arrived, I sat down with Chief Jeremy and summarized the results of my evaluation, explaining to him that I was of the opinion that all three cases were, indeed, related. I basically confirmed what he had already suspected, but I was able to do so based on proven methods of psychological and behavioral analysis.

We knew that all three victims were fair-skinned, of European descent, with long, dark hair. They were similar in size and stature, all being of petite build. They each had somewhat broad shoulders, which could be attributed to the fact that they were all swimmers. Each of the ladies was found on a beach of Lake Erie, the most easterly of the five Great Lakes. All had been swimming in the lake's water prior to their deaths. Positioned in a similar fashion, all were on their backs lying on a large slab of slate rock. Strangely, none of the victims displayed defensive wounds or showed signs of a struggle.

"Did they know their attacker?" I posed the question to Chief Jeremy. "At the very least, I believe they all held some level of trust."

The locations they were found were all considered remote areas by normal standards. The perpetrator went to great lengths to identify these locations or may have already been familiar with them. All were frequented during daylight hours by rock hounds and beach glass hunters, but by nightfall, all areas were considered off-limits by the locals. These locations allowed the victims to be secluded, yet also allowed for each of the deceased bodies to be found by the next morning's light. All three had been sexually assaulted. None were left with any verifiable DNA from their perpetrator; however, some results from Anna's forensic testing were still pending. Death by asphyxiation was determined to be their cause of death.

Lastly and quite deliberately, was the single red ribbon tied around each of their necks. All confirmed having been tied by a left-handed attacker.

The only thing that didn't make sense was that two of the victims were young college-aged girls. They belonged to their respective university swim teams. Anna, on the other hand, was a middle-aged woman who, although she looked young for her age, was well beyond the traditional college-age student. Therefore, she didn't match the profile of the other two in that respect. She didn't have a known affiliation with the local university, although there was one located in our community.

I said to Chief Jeremy, "A point of interest is that while scouring several of the information-sharing databases, I came across a couple of other cases with similar narratives. One is further west in Pennsylvania and another in Ohio. Both of these cases are unsolved. Both have occurred within the past five years. Both bodies were found along Lake Erie. I think we should take a closer look at them as well."

Chief Jeremy widened his eyes and raised his brows as he listened.

I explained that I felt strongly that all evidence should be examined by one single laboratory, utilizing one expert per discipline. When dealing with a serial murder investigation, we wanted to limit the number of labs and experts involved in order to maintain continuity of results. This would obviously require retesting of some or all of the evidence. I felt that this would confirm my findings and leave no room for doubt. If this was not possible, we at least needed to establish lines of communication between the labs to ensure all interested parties are sharing information pertinent to the investigation.

Chief Jeremy was in agreement and continued to discuss the best options for building the team of investigators. Chief Jeremy would take the lead with Officer Griffin acting as co-lead. It would be imperative to bring officials in from Ohio; each lead could designate additional support as necessary. It would be important to identify IT, administrative, and other support staff as well. If needed, we could effectively utilize some of the resources remotely versus in-house. I also recommended that a skilled trace evidence examiner be brought on board, where we could utilize their expertise in comparing trace evidence from victims. The goal would be to identify the commonalities among them. Although it didn't seem like much was left behind in all three cases, they may be able to find something that will reflect a "common environment" with which all of the victims were in contact. The examiner would be looking for this to repeat in objects in the offender's world, such as their vehicle, their residence, or even their clothing, Ultimately, this could connect the offender to the murders.

I pointed out that there were a number of issues to consider since this is now a multi-jurisdictional case. There may be variations in evidentiary and interview standards, search warrant requirements, and other investigative protocols that will prove significant when prosecuting the case, so we must ensure we are aware of these at all times. I expressed the importance of networking with all involved law enforcement and investigative agencies and cited multiple resources that would be at our disposal for those communications. I further pointed to the mechanisms I was able to use in my own analysis of the victims that proved integral in linking them together.

Chief Jeremy was grateful for my experiential knowledge, and although he hadn't led an investigation involving serial murders before, he had led some pretty complex, high-profile cases in the past. It was actually the stress and trauma of those high-profile cases that led him to return to his quiet little hometown of Ackerton.

Little did he realize that another prominent case, being this one, would find him here.

Chief Jeremy was eager to take on the challenge. I was glad because he was a good fit with his background as a competent homicide investigator and with his experience in directing the investigative process. As for me? He requested that I continue my assistance on the team. We both knew his request was merely a formality, since we both also knew it was my intent to stay should this turn out to be a serial matter.

Since Ackerton, Pennsylvania, was logistically located right in the middle of Duncan, New York, and Casperson, Ohio, we felt it was a good option to utilize this space to head up our operations. This was further supported by an initial geographical profile that identified the most probable area of offender residence to be within a 100-mile radius of Ackerton. I felt it could be even closer than that. Additionally, Ackerton was out of the limelight of mainstream media. It offered a bit of seclusion from the attention we ultimately expected to garner.

In closing our conversation, Chief Jeremy asked, "Would you mind briefing Officer Griffin for me?"

Since Colin and I had already arranged to meet with Fred that afternoon, I humbly obliged. This would require me to meet with him before we met with Fred.

As I drove back to town, I had an hour of solitude just to think. Knowing I would be staying in the area for an undetermined amount of time, I would have to make arrangements to see my children. My ex-husband and I worked pretty well together, so I really wasn't concerned about making it happen. What I was more concerned about was my professional relationship with Colin. That is exactly how it HAD to stay. I resolved to remain steadfast in this decision and was determined to keep things as straightforward and impersonal as possible. Although I didn't want to appear cold or callous, that may be the case since I knew this was going to require a delicate balance between emotions and professionalism.

Back in town, I met Colin at the Duncan Police Station, ready to brief him on the results of my findings, as well as, my and Chief Jeremy's meeting. He shared with me that the jurisdictional issue had been resolved and that it was determined that Anna's body was found within the authority of Duncan law enforcement. He explained that the county sheriff was pretty upset about the decision. Ultimately, it didn't much matter though, since Anna's case was now part of a multi-jurisdictional investigation.

"Maybe we can consider his involvement on the investigative team," I suggested.

Colin was in full agreement. "And speaking of the Sheriff, look what hit the news while you were away," Colin said as he held up the *Daily Disturber*.

The big bold headline read, **"Key Suspect Named in Anna Leone's Murder!"**

Of course, they named Fred right away, and they were far from shy with the decorative language they used to depict Fred and Anna's affair. I couldn't even bring myself to read the entire article and rolled my eyes as I tossed the paper onto the table.

Thinking that our conversation had concluded and we would be leaving to meet with Fred, I pushed my chair away from the table. It screeched across the floor, making an unbearable sound that sent shivers down my back. Cringing, I instinctively looked up to apologize, and I noticed that Colin was just sitting there … silently … staring at me. His eyes were fixed on me, almost as if he was in a trance. His gaze was one of admiration, mixed with a hint of sadness. I remembered that look from long ago. It was the look that made me fall into his arms time and time again. How easily my walls could come crashing down. It was in this moment that I realized that I had never stopped loving him. Chills crept up and down my spine. And suddenly, he broke the silence.

"Why? Why did you leave, Sonny?"

I immediately entered pure panic mode! So, I did as I typically did when I felt threatened … I ran. Jumping up from my chair, I grabbed my purse, and as I was fleeing out the door, I said, "I'll meet you at Emily and Fred's house."

Out the door I flew, acting oblivious to his inquiry. I don't even think I took the time to glance back at him as I was rushing away.

Once safely in my car, I could feel my heart racing as I tried to catch my breath.

"Holy shit! What just happened back there?" I thought to myself.

Meanwhile, in the back of my mind I could hear a little voice say, "You know if you stay, you are going to have to tell him."

I slumped in my seat and put both hands on the top of the steering wheel. Hanging my head between my arms, I closed my eyes in solitude. It had only been a half hour that I'd been in Colin's company, and I was already fully aware of how difficult it was going to be to maintain my professional composure.

CHAPTER 9

The Selfie

Sunday, July 14, 2024

Colin arrived at Emily and Fred's shortly after me. I had never actually been to their house before. Aside from needing a little TLC, it was actually quite homey. Emily led us to the dining room, where Fred was seated at the small, weathered wooden table. He sat, hands clasped in front of him, and peered up as we entered the room. Normally a robust and talkative kind of guy, he looked worn, with a sense of defeat. It was evident he hadn't paid much attention to his personal hygiene this particular morning … or in the previous few days for that matter. He spoke not a word and hung his head back down.

As we sat down at the table, Emily shuffled off to gather some refreshments. Before leaving the room, however, she encouraged Fred, "Go on, tell them, Fred. Tell them everything!"

Fred laboriously raised his head and spoke. "I didn't kill Anna. I could never hurt her."

He mumbled over his words, and with tear-filled eyes, he said, "I could never ... I loved her."

Colin and I looked at each other in astonishment. Not what I was expecting to hear at all. "You loved her?" I asked.

Fred confessed that he had been having an affair with Anna for well over six months. It started out as a relationship of convenience, meant only to fill each other's physical needs—no commitment, no intimacy, no emotional attachment. At a time when Fred was experiencing feelings of mediocrity in his life, Anna sparked his desire to feel alive. She could offer him a sultry and provocative partner, willing to play out nearly any role he had previously only ever fantasized about. Those adventuresome days were long gone between him and Emily, so by filling this void, he could achieve freedom from the constraints of a life he *thought* he no longer wanted.

"But what could Anna have possibly gotten out of the deal?" I thought to myself. "Fred was simply not her type. Not her type at all! Not physically ... not professionally ... not even intellectually. What WAS the attraction?"

Fred must have been reading the look on my face because he assured us that Anna, too, received benefits from their union. While she was initially drawn in by his attention and flattery, having a late-night drinking buddy and an at-will booty call were conducive to her, then-current needs. Anna was not looking for another marriage. She was more than financially comfortable, having drawn a large part of her wealth from her previous marriages. There was nothing she really wanted ... other than, maybe, a boy toy. Fred could fulfill that role while representing everything she was not. He was rough around the edges with a raw, rugged strength. For her, he was the guy from the wrong side of the tracks ... the one her mother warned her about. Fred was Anna's dirty little secret.

But Fred was also *safe* for Anna. His marital status offered seductive simplicity, and hiding together in the shadows only added a layer of thrill and mystique to their already sordid affair. In layman's terms, it was exciting. She could portray herself as available to the outside world while having the benefits of a relationship behind closed doors.

Somewhere along the line, however, something unexpected happened. They both began to have genuine feelings for one another. And though they were polar opposites, their opposing values drew them even closer together. Fred assured us that they had been in a good place. Neither wanted, or needed, a formal commitment. They were both content with what they had, with no strings attached. I sat patiently listening, and as I tried to wrap my head around the context of their relationship, I couldn't help but think about Anna.

"If she were sitting with us at this moment, what would she have had to say about Fred? Was she really that content?"

"And poor, poor Emily. I can't even begin to imagine how she was processing all of this. She was not only betrayed by her husband; she was betrayed by her friend too."

This thought only raised another question.

"What about Emily? I wondered when she actually found out about Fred and Anna's affair. She *does* have motive," I thought. "It doesn't always have to be a man committing these types of crimes."

Fred continued to talk, but his voice was muddled by these incessant thoughts going through my mind. "Could it be possible that Emily is somehow tied to the other two victims?"

"No! Now, I'm just thinking crazy thoughts. There is no way that Emily could be capable of something so egregious."

"Then again," I thought as it struck me, "she *is* left-hand dominant."

As my mind continued to ponder, the ceiling light began to flicker. At first, it was a single flash, followed by two, and then more. Before we knew it, a steady stream of flashing light was strobing above our heads. I had never seen anything like it. It went on for several minutes, and as quickly as it started, it stopped. We all just sat there staring at one another, not quite sure what to make of it.

Fred assured us that nothing like that had ever happened before. He was doubtful that there was any type of electrical issue, but still, he said he would have it checked out. I thought the whole event was eerily odd, as more crazy thoughts entered my mind.

"Maybe it was Anna, trying to tell us what really happened."

As Fred paused, I could tell that the look in his eyes was genuine. I was far from being any fan of his, but putting all personal feelings aside, it was evident that he was authentically heartbroken over Anna's death. To compound those emotions even further, he was also experiencing considerable anguish over his transgressions. Neither he nor Anna stopped to consider what this might do to his wife and Anna's friend. They didn't plan on getting caught. No one ever does when they find themselves trapped in a lover's triangle. He expressed grievous sorrow for the pain he had brought upon Emily. And as she re-entered the room, with refreshments in hand, I could see the anguish on her face as well. I had no doubt that she had been listening in on much of our conversation. And as she joined us at the table, she looked at me with a pitifully sad and abandoned look on her face.

"It's ok, Sonny. I know all the nasty details. Maybe I'm still in shock over everything, but for now, I'm still standing, and I will continue to stand by my Fred."

I nodded a formal acceptance as I thought to myself in awe. Over all these years, I'd only ever viewed Emily as being little more than a helplessly weak, abused housewife. But looking at her in this moment, I saw an uncommon strength. She had a strength that exuded from her as she navigated this tragedy with loyalty and grace.

But still, everyone is a suspect … until they're not.

As the conversation continued, Fred shared his alibi regarding his whereabouts at the time of Anna's death. He had spent the afternoon fishing with a couple of buddies, enjoyed dinner and drinks at a local club, and then joined an impromptu four-wheeler gathering afterward. He arrived home around 5:00 a.m. on the morning Anna's body was found. Colin confirmed that his story was consistent with the version Sheriff Howard had previously corroborated. Colin also went on to explain that prior to coming to our meeting, he had followed up on the semen sample they had retrieved from Anna's body. The findings were inconclusive due to cross-contamination and how the sample was taken. So, there would be no DNA evidence linking Fred to Anna, romantically or otherwise. Unless, of course, his DNA turned up elsewhere in the investigation.

Colin and I agreed that Fred was not a likely suspect. At least not for now. However, we cautioned him that nothing was set in stone and should additional evidence be uncovered that links him to the crime, we would be back. If we did have to come back, we might not be so forgiving. With him seemingly out of the woods, I diverted my attention to Anna's activities and behavior in the days leading up to her murder.

"Had she said anything that seemed odd? What was she doing during those days? Were you aware of any of her other associations?" I implored Fred to give me as many details as possible.

Fred had indicated that he was supposed to meet up with Anna later that evening. During the day, they had sent one another a number of graphically revealing photos and sexually explicit text messages in anticipation of that meeting. By evening, his messages to her had gone unanswered. He did what he could to avoid going home as long as he could, half expecting Anna to reach out to him in the middle of the night as she sometimes did. But that communication never came.

The police had not been privy to this information since Fred had a separate cell phone specifically designated for his and Anna's conversations. He had not told the police about it in anticipation of turning it over through his lawyer … but then he was released.

"Weren't you the least bit concerned when your messages went unanswered?" I asked.

"I felt a little rejected actually. But then I figured she must have just fallen asleep after her workout," Fred replied.

Fred went on to explain that Anna had been preparing to participate in a triathlon. He knew she had been swimming laps at the university swimming pool earlier in the day. She had a fairly strict routine. The last message he received was around 6:30 p.m. as he was heading over to the Fisherman's Club.

I encouraged him, as I said, "Was there anything else? Anything at all that you can think of that you may not have thought of before? No matter how small you may think it is. It could be important."

He pursed his lips and slowly shook his head back and forth to indicate a negative response. But then, his expression changed. His eyes widened.

"The picture!" he exclaimed.

He pulled a phone out of his pocket and scrolled across the screen. He held the phone out to show me.

"She sent me this selfie. It was attached to her last message."

I held the phone in my hand and gave the screen a long glance. It was a headshot of Anna puckering her voluptuously pouty lips. Her wet hair draped gently around her shoulders, creating a sultry frame for her uninhibited expression. The only thing missing was an equally seductive background. Instead, one could see the crystal-clear water of the swimming pool. Benches lined the wall with massive windows above them. The exit door was also in view. And as I drew the phone closer to my eyes, there appeared to be a figure of a person in the doorway. It was not clearly visible, so it was difficult to discern whether it was a male or female figure. Though difficult to distinguish, maybe through forensic software we could get a clearer view. Colin and I agreed it was a long shot, but I asked Fred if we could keep his phone in order to retrieve the photo.

Fred's initial reaction was to withhold his phone as he snatched it out of my hands. One look from Emily's darting eyes, however, quickly changed his mind. He reluctantly agreed on the condition that no one, other than Colin and I, would have access to it and its contents. We agreed, with the exception of the photo in question. Although we knew we could gain access in other ways, specifically through legal channels, we appreciated that Fred was being as candid and forthright as he was. And in all reality, for the amount of time it would take to obtain a court order, he could easily erase the data and mysteriously *lose* the phone. Taking this into consideration and out of the utmost respect for Emily, this was the best-case scenario.

Finishing up our visit, my mind wandered back to that impossible question.

"What about Emily? Could she have somehow gotten caught up in a jealous rage and taken her anger out on Anna?"

I shuddered to think of the possibility. I reminded myself that this was the work of a serial killer. Emily would have no motive for killing the other two victims.

At least none that I knew of.

CHAPTER 10

The Witness

Friday, July 19, 2024

The week flew by in a chaotic mess. My days were consumed with commuting to Ackerton, where I was working well into the evenings. I knew that today would be no different, but I had already decided to spend it locally, in Duncan. It was my intention to dissect every witness statement specific to Anna's case. In addition, Sheriff Howard, from the county, had turned additional records over to the Duncan PD. I would focus my attention on this additional information as well.

In anticipation of my day, I decided to take my time getting to the police station. I needed a little reprieve for myself. I would take some time for Sonya. If even just for a couple hours, I craved a moment to declutter my brain and find some clarity in all this chaos. What better way to do it than with a morning drive through the fresh country air?

Mom stored a cute little convertible in her garage. It was a silver, two-door VW Beetle. She called her, "Betty the Bug."

"I think today would be a great day to take Betty for a spin," I thought to myself.

So off we went, the little Bug and I, out to explore the countryside on this clear and sunny Friday morning. I lowered the roof and put my sunglasses on. Together, we whizzed off into the breeze on the open winding roads. With my hair flying freely past my shoulders, we had no direction. For this brief time, we had no cares. Soon enough, however, I found myself on an old, though quite familiar, road.

I hadn't driven this way in so many years. Yet, it seemed like yesterday. "Had I just instinctively driven here?" I thought to myself.

Many were the nights that Colin and I would travel this route. We'd randomly pull off the beaten path to steal a kiss or two. He'd lay a blanket down in the cool, green grass surrounded by the mighty oak trees. Or maybe we'd find ourselves among the evergreens with a clear patch, open to the sky. We'd lie on our backs for hours gazing up at the heavens, listening to the sounds of the crickets and the toads, and talking about our futures ... our hopes, wishes, and dreams. Those nights that we spent lying in each other's arms, or simply holding each other's hand, dimmed out the reality of the commotion around us. It was as if no one else existed. Time stood still in our own little world. It was us and a million stars, all alone, in the darkness of the night.

Nothing along this road seemed to have changed, yet nothing stayed the same.

Lost in my thoughts, which was becoming quite the norm these days, I had also lost track of time. Before I realized it, I was back in town and pulling into the parking lot of the Duncan Police Station. It is amazing how the human mind works. Here, I hadn't been on that road in at least twenty years. I completely forgot it ever existed. Until today. And now I had remembered it like the back of my hand.

Colin had stepped out for the afternoon with his own investigative work to do. He had planned to follow up with neighborhood residents who lived on the road that led to the beach where Anna was found. He had hoped to identify the perpetrators' vehicle from one of their webcams. His absence from the office was actually a relief after how I had run out on him earlier in the week. Although, I had to admit that I would miss not getting a glimpse of him.

After entering the precinct, an officer led me to Colin's office. "Feel free to use the conference table in here. Everything you need should be right there," as he pointed to the end of the table.

I thanked him as he departed and left me to my own devices.

I stood in silence and glanced around the room. On the corner of his faux-wood desk sat the remnants of his very early-morning coffee. As I stared at the half-empty cup, I chuckled at the inscription thereupon: *Not Yo' Average Crime Solver!*

"A very Colin-like quote," I thought to myself. Because there was certainly nothing average about him.

On the other side of his coffee cup lay a laptop, and beyond that stood an old, familiar lamp.

"Is that the lamp *I gave to him*?"

I stepped closer and extended my hand to caress the top of the brass-plated eagle that stood proudly above the shade.

"Wow. It sure was."

It was a gift I had given to him our last Christmas together. It really was a majestic piece. Monetarily, it held little value, though, so I couldn't help but smile at the thought that he may have kept it around for its nostalgic value.

My attention shifted back to the conference table. There lay a chaotic mess of sticky notes scattered about. I couldn't help but laugh again. He was a man after my own heart. My whole world revolved around those trusty little tacky notepads. I could not function in my world without them.

I was soon distracted by the faint buzzing of the fluorescent lighting above. It added to the institutional feel around the room. While the walls were skillfully plastered with many awards and recognitions, something seemed to be missing. I stood staunchly and glanced around once again. I noticed what was amiss. The room was completely devoid of any kind of photos. It was so professional and so impersonal at the same time. I almost felt a little sad for him. A flicker of the lights captured my attention and reminded me that it was time to refocus and get to work.

Sitting down at the table, there were well over one hundred witness statements lying before me; as I filtered through them, one by one, none really captured my eye. They didn't appear to have much substance that would help with the investigation.

"We met for lunch a week before her death." Or,

"I passed by her on the street." Or,

"She waved to me from her car."

This was the general consensus. I continued trolling through the statements until finally, I came across one that grabbed my attention. Signed by a local woman, she indicated that they swam together. An alarm went off in my head.

"WAIT! What? They swam together? This is the one I want to talk to!" I said to myself.

Out the door I flew. On my way to 4 Jackson Street, hoping to speak with Valerie Kline.

Valerie was an older woman, in her early 60s. With glistening gray hair, her sophisticated bob fell softly around her face. She was well put together, with a unique fashion sense that was all her own. She greeted me in the doorway, and after the initial introduction, ushered me to take a seat on the glider swing on her front porch. I explained that I had read her statement and wished for her to tell me more. I wanted to know how well she and Anna knew each other.

Valerie explained that they didn't know each other well and that they really hadn't swum *together* like it was implied in her statement. She explained that they were more of acquaintances who happened to swim at the same time at the college. I was convinced that I still wanted to hear exactly what happened or what she had observed, in her own words. She was much obliged at my interest and stated:

"I had gone to the university swimming pool on the afternoon of June 21st. I didn't know Anna personally, but I knew who she was from seeing her there. She arrived around, I'd say, 4:30 in the afternoon. She jumped in the pool and started her workout right away. She spent a couple of hours swimming a variety of different laps and drills. It's what she always did. Sometimes, at the end of her workout, we would share a bit of small talk. But not on this day. This day she was very preoccupied with her phone, texting and taking pictures of herself … giggling and taking more photos. She left the pool at about 6:45 p.m., and that was the last I ever saw of her."

I explained to Valerie that I was interested in hearing about anyone else that may have been at the pool that day. "Please, take a moment to think hard about who you may have seen."

Valerie pointed out that they were the only two who were there that afternoon. "I like to go on Friday afternoons. There is never anybody there on Fridays."

"Think hard, Valerie. This is really important. Did you notice **anyone** else at all?" I pressed.

Valerie squinted her eyes and pursed her lips, gesturing as though she was thinking as hard as she could. "Hmmmmmm, well, there was a man. But only for a moment."

"A man?" I asked.

"Yes. But I didn't get a good look at him. I think he was there looking for someone. I noticed him in the doorway, but he was only there for a moment. I assumed whoever he was looking for wasn't there, because he turned and left."

"What do you remember about this man?" I persisted.

"Not much. He was an older gentleman … skinny … tall maybe … dark clothing. It's hard to say because I really didn't pay much attention to him."

"Go on," I prodded.

"Like I said, I didn't get a good look at him. He wasn't there for long." Valerie was clutching her head in a gesture that implied she was trying to think.

"Do you think this could have been her killer? The newspaper said she was murdered." Valerie was clearly anxious as she tried to recall her memory.

I reassured her that I was only looking for additional witnesses. I handed her my card and thanked her for her time, firmly encouraging her to contact me if there were any other details she could think of. She nodded, and as I turned to walk away, she called out to me,

"Wait! His eyes! There was something about his eyes!"

Questioning her comment, I turned to her and asked, "His eyes? What do you mean?"

She replied. "I'm not sure. They seemed empty or something."

"How so?" I asked.

She recalled, "Well, he wore sunglasses. He lifted them at one point, and his eyes looked so dark and hollow. Even from a distance I noticed it."

A shiver went down my spine. I've seen those eyes before ... eyes that are impenetrable, callous, and cold. It's almost like there is nothing behind them. For not saying much, she certainly had a lot to say!

Valerie hadn't mentioned anyone else at the swimming pool in her original statement. That statement had been bare-bones brief. Now, however, she had definitively placed Anna at the university swimming pool shortly before her death. From the selfie that Fred received, there really was no way to ascertain if it had been sent right when the photo was snapped or not. Without Anna's telephone, which has yet to turn up, we had no way of knowing when the photo Fred received had actually been taken. But now, there were strong indications that Fred's selfie coincided with Valerie's timing of events. Valerie may very well have been the last one to see Anna alive. And, Fred was likely the last one to be in contact with her ... aside from the killer, that is.

"That was it!" I thought to myself. "THAT was the connection!"

We knew they were all swimmers. We knew they all had regular access to a swimming pool located at a facility of higher education. *THIS* has got to be how the perpetrator had gained access to his victims. This has to be where he was finding them. Everything, somehow, seemed to revolve around these college swimming pools. But they ended up at a beach on Lake Erie. We knew the victims drove their own cars because their cars were found at each of the crime scenes.

"Were they somehow forced to go? With no defensive wounds, it would seem that they went willingly." I couldn't imagine how he would have been able to gain their trust. "Could they have known him?" I wondered.

I was excited at the developing theory. I knew I was on the right path. It was definitely an angle I was going to pursue. I'd made a point to add a review of the campus videos to my list of things to do. I'd also ask Colin to followup with any video cameras on the route between the university pool and the location where her body was found. For now, though, I would call it a day.

Closing the car door, thoughts of relaxing in a hot soapy tub with a tall glass of Pinot Noir danced in my head.

The short-lived thought was shattered when suddenly, my phone rang. Lifting it to my ear, I heard the distinct voice of Chief Jeremy. My presence was requested at an impromptu dinner to finalize details for our investigative team kickoff meeting scheduled for Monday morning.

I acknowledged I would be there.

"And bring Officer Griffin with you too!" Chief Jeremy said.

CLICK went the phone before I had a chance to respond!

"Oh boy!" I thought. "This should be interesting."

CHAPTER 11

The Kiss

The drive was definitely awkward. Colin had insisted that we ride together since we were expecting bad weather later in the evening. During the entire thirty-minute ride, I anticipated that Colin would revisit his question as to why I had left town all those years ago. My stomach was churning incessantly. But instead, we mostly stuck to updating each other on our activities of the day. I shared my theory on how the perpetrator might be selecting his or her victims and potentially gaining access to them.

Although we had previously determined that Fred was an unlikely suspect, he and Emily would both continue to linger in a far-off corner of my mind. For the most part, however, I explained that I was leaning toward the idea that our perp was a lone-acting male. I was fairly convinced we were dealing with a male, and I would refer to him as such, unless proven otherwise during the course of the investigation.

He has a job that requires travel. At minimum, he travels along the Lake Erie shoreline. It's also possible that his travel may extend throughout the east coast or beyond. He is somehow affiliated with the swimming industry. Maybe he is a coach or a recruiter of some sort. Maybe he even presents himself as a like-minded athlete.

Colin shared some insights on follow-up work he had done as well. He had spent the earlier part of the day attempting to locate web cams that may have recorded the perpetrator's vehicle in the location of the beach entrance on the day of the murder. He was able to determine that several recordings held potential evidence of the perp. He had the digital footage forwarded to his cell phone, which he allowed me to view.

In these videos, Anna's vehicle could be seen traveling north down the entrance road toward the beach. In a second video, the resident who resided adjacent to the parking entrance was able to retrieve video that showed Anna parking her vehicle, exiting, and being greeted by an unknown figure. The figure appeared to be that of a male. Further review of video footage showed that the male figure previously drove past the parking entrance and parked out of camera view. The individual then walked back into view of the video, where Anna was met upon her arrival. They stood by Anna's vehicle briefly talking. Nothing about their conversation seemed out of the ordinary. Anna was dressed in her one-piece blue bathing suit with a pair of shorts. She reached into her car for a towel before heading toward the lake. Another short clip showed Anna and the figure walking toward the water until they were out of view. The video clips clocked Anna's arrival at the beach at 7:12 p.m. There was no video showing the figure's departure from the area.

Interestingly, the vehicle in question appeared to be a vintage-style model. It was black in color with deep tinting on the windows. Unfortunately, any truly identifying information was not readable on the videos. Either the angle was wrong or the recording was too far away. I doubted that even with identification software, we would get a definite ID of the license, make, or model.

Another notable result of his day included a conversation he had with the forensics lab. Some of the toxicology results had come back. Apparently, they found traces of vecuronium bromide in Anna's system.

My heart dropped. I knew exactly what that meant. Having dealt with this drug in the past, I shared with Colin the impact of its use.

"Vecuronium bromide is a paralytic agent, primarily used during surgery to induce muscle relaxation and paralysis. Anesthesiologists typically employ its use, along with deep sedation, to prevent surgical patients from being aware while they are in a paralyzed state. Vecuronium does not act as an analgesic or sedative.

Meaning, it does **not** prevent pain or put the patient to sleep. Administered alone, the patient cannot speak or move but will be fully aware of pain and everything going on around them. It is a rapid-onset medication with a time to onset of sixty seconds. Its effects can last 30-40 minutes without additional dosing, and it is administered intravenously."

I continued, "This would explain the bruising and small pinprick found on Anna's right leg."

This news was absolutely devastating. It was both devastating *and* terrifying. My mind could not fathom what type of monster would use such tactics on their victim.

Imagine lying there, eyes wide open, unable to speak or move.

Imagine that while you are lying there, you are fully aware of everything that is happening around you.

Now *imagine* that you can hear your perpetrator's every word and feel every touch. There is nothing you can do to fend him off.

Imagine being able to feel pain and not be able to react or scream. You know you are going to die, and there is nothing you can do to save yourself.

No matter what I had ever thought of Anna personally, she did not deserve to die in this cruel and inhumane way. No one does.

With this new information came new theories. One consideration was that of control. The use of a paralytic drug gives the perp maximum control over every aspect of another human being's fate. Conscious but incapacitated.

He is likely aroused by submissive behavior, which is marked by their inability to move. At the same time, by keeping the victim aware, he can imagine the victim as a willing partner.

Our perp was also someone who enjoyed the adrenaline rush of fear, in a magnified way. In a normal person, adrenaline will race through their veins in high-stakes situations. This gives them a high or a rush. For some, it's a burst of energy. Our perp has likely had repeated exposure to sexually explicit and terrifying situations. Through time and circumstance, his biological response to this adrenaline rush has equated to intense sexual arousal. While anyone's biological response to a threat naturally spikes the adrenaline, for our perp, this induces a euphoric state so intense that he seeks it out over and over again … each time trying to reach a newer, more intense climax. It all comes down to thrill seeking, and I liken this to someone who loves to watch scary movies. It is the adrenaline rush of fear that causes them to continue to seek them out over and over again.

In his twisted and sick mind, our perp may be trying to recreate that pleasurable feeling for his victim. At the same time, watching the terror mount in their eyes is extremely gratifying for him. It serves as the appetizer before his next meal.

We now had another matter to consider, and that was where he may be getting access to the drug. Vecuronium is developed and researched by both pharmaceutical companies and institutions of higher education. Our perp has a connection with one, or the other, or both.

We arrived at the restaurant, and I couldn't decide whether I wanted to head straight for the bathroom and throw up or sit down and guzzle a nice, tall glass of wine. My vivid imagination tends to visualize things; the visual of Anna being assaulted, fully aware, and unable to fight back had really rattled my nerves. Chief Jeremy was settled and waiting for us to arrive, so we headed straight for the table in the far corner where he was seated.

Wine it was.

Overall, our dinner meeting was productive, and we agreed on several key talking points for our meeting on Monday. We had settled on the main players for the team; Chief Jeremy noted that the Chattacoin County Sheriff had been invited, but as of the time of our dinner, had not responded that he would be in attendance. Colin assumed he was upset about losing jurisdiction on Anna's case, but at this point, it was moot. Hers was now a federal matter.

Just as we had finished our discussion, Chief Jeremy received an urgent phone call. He apologetically excused himself but assured us it couldn't be helped. So, there we were, Colin and I, alone in each other's company. By this point, I was on my third glass of wine and starting to feel much more relaxed than I normally had in his presence.

Colin had sensed my uneasiness earlier in the evening. I can typically take things in stride, but Anna's death, being so personal, was really bothering me. I knew her. And the thought of her suffering the way I believed she had was very upsetting. He tried his hardest to keep things light after Chief Jeremy left. I was grateful to him for that. And for the first time since I had arrived back in Duncan, I felt like we were moving beyond the uneasy presence we normally felt. I actually sensed that we were making a connection and beginning to enjoy each other's company … like two strangers meeting for the first time. I suppose the ambience of the restaurant lent itself to the transpiring mood as well. With the lights dimmed way down low and candles flickering gracefully, mouth-watering aromas filled the air. And the wine. Let's not forget the wine.

Finishing my third glass, I peered out the window in anticipation that we would soon be leaving. To my surprise, my view outside was met by streams of water trickling down to the ground. I had forgotten that the weather forecast had been calling for a storm, and it was about to get pretty fierce. Soon, a heavy pitter-patter began tapping against the windows. Then, a flickering

107

light show began. It brightened the clouds as thundering acoustics reverberated across the sky. The wind picked up, and the heavy pattering quickly turned into a pounding downpour. Checking the forecast on his phone, Colin decided it would be safer for us to wait out the worst of it before heading home. It was a great excuse to order *just one more round.*

I should have known better. All inhibitions go out the door with alcohol. I wasn't a seasoned drinker, and four glasses of wine was well beyond my limit. But I told myself that after the day I had, it was OK. So, with the storm beating relentlessly down upon the old tin roof of the building, we sought refuge in each other's company ... never getting too personal, yet allowing for some harmless, flirtatious fun. I couldn't deny that I felt tantalizingly aroused. And my guess is that Colin felt it too.

It was about 10 p.m. when the worst of the storm had passed. We decided it would be best to get out while the going was good. Even though the rain was still coming down, the lightning and thunder had subsided, and the wind had all but gone.

Together we left the restaurant, walking swiftly to get out of the rain. Then, all of a sudden, he stopped me. I was a couple of steps in front of him when he placed his hand on my shoulder to slow my stride. Colin slowly turned me around to face him. I tried to resist, but his towering presence was just too much to deny. Pushing my back up against a nearby light pole, he gently leaned his body against mine. I could feel his intense power over my weightless frame. With one arm resting on the pole above my head, he placed the forefinger of his other hand under my chin and gently lifted my face to meet his gaze. I fell instantly and hopelessly under the enchantment of his pale blue eyes … eyes that were opened wide and filled with lust. As my heartbeat quickened and my breaths grew deeper, he leaned in even closer. Pressing more firmly against me, he placed his soft, moist lips upon mine. He held that kiss … that hot, breathy kiss … as the droplets of rain slid sensually down my forehead and over my cheeks. There we were, sharing one breath, in one abiding and passionate moment.

Colin slowly drew his face away and stared tenderly into my eyes. He was searching for my acceptance or rejection of the impassioned kiss we had just shared. With the amber glow of the street lamp highlighting his masculine features, I was powerless under his spell ...

… He had kissed me like I wanted to be kissed.

… He had kissed me like no man had ever kissed me before.

… I melted in his embrace.

CHAPTER 12

Feather In The Wind

Saturday, July 20, 2024

"Was it all just a dream?" I said softly under my breath.

I lay in bed with the morning breeze caressing my cheek. The sheets were light and soft and smelled of freshly cleaned linen. I observed the curtains drifting softly through the air and enjoyed awakening to the starlings as they chirped a morning serenade. I slowly stretched my arms above my head. I could feel a gentle release down the length of my entire spine.

Inhaling deeply, then releasing my breath in a sigh of relief, I thought to myself, "It was **not** just a dream." I smiled.

My eyes shifted toward the door. Colin stood sturdily, leaning against the frame as if he were holding the entire structure in place. He had been staring at me with a look of adoration in his eyes. His hair was disheveled, and sporting a morning shadow on his chin, he remained relaxed in the most unassuming way.

He tilted his head and grinned as he said, "Good morning, Sunshine. Sleep well?"

He looked so demure in his boxer briefs as he glided across the floor. In his hands he carried two fresh, hot cups of cappuccino.

No. It hadn't been a dream at all.

"Good morning." I responded and smiled back.

The barrier was now broken. My wall was torn down, and there was no turning back. Colin slid into the bed next to me, and while handing me my cup, he snuggled in to gently kiss my neck. The touch of his warm breath sent a shiver down my spine.

"You know, we have a lot of lost time to make up for," he said.

I nodded in agreement, with a bashful grin. We sat together, relishing in the moment, and sipping from our steaming cups. "Where would we go from here?" swirled around in my head.

I had broken my golden rule. I never dated anyone I worked with. At least not until now. Colin was the exception. We spent the remainder of the morning talking about different scenarios of how we might move forward. We didn't need to discuss whether or not we would move forward; the connection was far too strong to deny. But we had a lot to consider, and ultimately, we agreed that we would keep our personal relationship private ... at least for the time being.

By the time I left Colin's, it was already early afternoon. Having not been home since the day before, I felt like an unruly teen sneaking in from a late night out. Of course, as I walked in the door, I was greeted by my mother.

"Doing the walk of shame?" she asked.

"Don't ask," I strongly suggested as I smiled under my breath.

With eyebrows raised and a tilt of her head, she didn't speak another word. She merely gave me a side eye and a crooked grin. I proceeded directly to my bedroom.

After a much-needed shower, I returned downstairs and sat with Mom for a while. I knew the anticipation was killing her, so I confided that I had been at Colin's the night before. I didn't go into all the details; I didn't need to. She was ecstatic at the thought of us rekindling a relationship. She always liked Colin ... and she loved

Colin and me together. She never understood why I left town the way I did. Of course, no one did ... because no one knew my secret.

I cautioned Mom that Colin and I had lost a lot of years. We were not the same people we used to be. While our attraction was undisputed, we had a lot of catching up to do and were remaining open to see where this may lead ... or not lead. Either way, I knew I had her support. I always had her unending support.

With a hug and a kiss, I told her I wouldn't see her until the next morning. I had plans to return to Colin's later. But first, there were some errands I needed to take care of. And, off I went.

After completing my errands, it was early evening by the time I found myself headed in the direction of the crime scene where Anna had been found. I loved the beach when I was dressed appropriately; however, I was not a fan of the gritty sand finding its way beneath my clothing or in my shoes. I guess it was a small sacrifice to make in order to get up close and personal with the scene of the crime. It was important that I understood the layout of the land and visualized what may have occurred. What I already knew had painted a rather grim and graphic image in my mind. This visit would serve to fill in the backdrop for that image and help me to recreate Anna's final moments. Together, with my visitations to the other two crime scenes, I'd hoped to establish even more real-life patterns that would eventually lead us to their killer.

Her body had been found on the backshore of a small beach on Lake Erie. The backshore is the stretch of sand that remains outside of the water. It only gets covered during exceptionally high tides, which might occur during heavy rains or other adverse weather conditions. The exact location where her body had been found was atop a large slab of slate, much like the others. Surrounded by whisps of tall wild grass, the view of the water's edge was moderately obscured. She was a considerable distance from the waterline, yet we knew she had been in the lake water. Various samples of skin and hair taken during the autopsy confirmed that she had been swimming in the lake. That seemed odd since we knew she had, not long before, been swimming in a chlorinated pool.

"Why would she come for a swim at the lake after finishing her workout in a nice clean pool while knowing she had a romantic rendezvous to get ready for?" I thought to myself.

It just didn't make sense and confirmed to me the notion that this lake visit was more of an impromptu detour than a planned trip.

"The perpetrator lured her here." And he lured her here right after she had been at the pool." I was sure of this.

"But how? What did he use for bait?"

The mystery man from the pool had become more and more of interest to me.

As I stood there, I pictured Anna's body on the cold, gray slab. Imagining how she lay there, both motionless and fully aware, I envisioned her fear. I was having a difficult time coming to terms with the agony she must have felt while lying in that paralytic state and thinking about what she must have endured as that monster stole her last breath away. Apparently, she had been found with her one-piece suit tangled around her ankles.

As I exhaled, I could feel Anna's presence. I couldn't explain it, but I knew she was there. Standing right next to me.

"I'll find him, Anna. I'll find whoever did this to you." I spoke aloud to her.

Standing in silence, I noticed a lone white feather floating gently through the air. I instinctively looked toward the sky, searching for its owner. There were no birds in sight. Gently gliding on the breeze, it swayed back and forth until finally coming to rest on the limb of a small flowering plant, right in front of me. Notoriously symbolic of the presence of an angel, I thought to myself that the feather must surely be a sign from Anna. It was confirmation that she was there.

I couldn't help but notice that the sun was setting in the background. It would have been much like this the night that Anna died. Anywhere else, this would be a magnificent and glorious view. But here, it was like a tiny ball of fire, illuminating a bloody sky. I could never unsee the visions I had imagined in this place.

I refocused my sight on what was important. I crouched down to admire the little treasure before me. As I did, a glint of light caught my eye. I peered closer in the direction that it had come from. Not noticing anything out of the ordinary, my attention gravitated back to the feather. Again, a glimmer flashed. I caught it from the corner of my eye. For a moment I thought I may have imagined it, but now I was sure something was there. The sun's reflection was pointing the way. But what was it?

I perched myself on the rock, in a position that I thought the perp or Anna may have been sitting in. When I saw nothing, I repositioned myself. And then, I positioned again. Slowly scoping the area around me, there it was. I had caught another glimpse of the glinting flash and found the source of light. About three feet from me, tucked away in a crevice of the rocks and dusted with a covering of sand, was a cell phone. Camouflaged by the tiny grains, its golden hue blended in perfectly with the coloring of the case. That was until the sun's ray caught its tiny edge.

I was jumping from within from a combination of excitement and anticipation.

"Oh my gosh! Could this be Anna's missing phone?"

I carefully collected the specimen and placed it in a baggie. I always carried baggies on me, for just this very reason. Realizing it may be a coincidental find, completely unrelated to the case, I would remain hopeful for a connection and treat it as all other evidence is treated. As much as I wanted to open it up and look inside, I pushed the temptation away so as not to risk the integrity of the forensic testing.

It really was by chance that it had caught my eye in the first place. My gut told me it was no coincidence, though. Considering all the law enforcement that had scoured the area and not found it, I truly felt that it was Anna who led me. First the feather, and then the reflection from the sun. Strangely, though, it was when the sun was going to sleep for the evening that it had just enough spark to light the way.

"Not strange at all," I thought to myself. "*Anna* was lighting the way."

In contemplating the light, I hadn't noticed that the sky was rapidly turning gray; it would soon be completely black as the sun fell into the horizon. Recognizing that I was out there all alone caused me to unleash a chilling shiver. Of all the fears there are in this world, mine was of being surrounded by darkness.

"Go figure. A criminal profiler who's afraid of the dark," I thought to myself. But I knew I needed to get out of there, lest I be swallowed by the shadows.

After a quick stop at the forensics lab, I headed back to Colin's, where he greeted me at the front door. In hand, with a glass of pinot noir, he knew how I loved a medium-bodied wine with hints of cherry and raspberry.

He kissed me on the forehead as he led me through the house, out onto the veranda. The open-air patio served as a natural transition between the warm furnishings of his home and the outdoor entertainment space. It wrapped around the residence, reminiscent of an old Southern plantation, complete with pillars that supported a second veranda on the level above. It truly was a magnificent structure. Although not the typical architecture seen in this area of the country, it was at home on this vast piece of property.

Built in the mid-1800s, there is no doubt that it belonged to a family of considerable wealth. The expansive view of the countryside was even more spectacular. Rolling green pastures, dotted with alyssum, hollyhocks, and sunflowers, extending as far as the eye could see. The smell of fresh lavender and mint filled the air. Sitting high atop a hill, the dips and sways of the landscape continued into the distance to the north until they met the border of the dark blue waters of Lake Erie. Sunsets must surely be gorgeous from this side of the home.

Sitting down with this breathtaking backdrop, we sat silently, sipping our wine and taking in the fresh, clean scents of summer. I knew that before I got too used to this little piece of heaven, I would have to confide in him about the real reason I had left Duncan so many years before. Sitting in his quiet presence, I looked into his eyes. Hesitantly, I spoke … in a nervous but serious tone.

"Colin … I know I owe you an explanation."

He quickly interrupted, "It's ok, Sonny," as he reached across the table to clasp onto my hand. "We can talk about this when you are ready … in your own time."

His words comforted me and made me feel at ease. I knew he had a kind heart and would listen with an open mind. I felt the mood was right. I felt the time was right now.

CHAPTER 13

The Secret

Saturday, July 20, 2024

"I'm ready," I said to Colin. "I'm ready to share with you why I left Duncan."

Colin sat up in his chair and looked at me with concern on his face. "Are you sure?"

"I'm sure," I said. "I have kept this secret for twenty years. I can't keep this from you any longer."

I paused, took a deep breath, and then continued, "It all started the night you graduated from college. Do you remember that night?"

Colin responded, "Yes, Sonny. I'll never forget it. I even remember you had on that cute little flowered dress. It had little red bows on it. I loved those bows."

"I did," I said in response. Little did he know, I had come to hate and resent that dress forever.

He continued, "We had an argument that night. I think that was the last time I ever saw you. I was completely heartbroken."

I nodded in agreement. I recalled how we had been *downtown* celebrating graduation with all our friends that evening. Recollecting this college-town happening place, that five-square-block area was home to at least a dozen bars and pubs. Many memories were made in that small little footprint in the center of this neighboring Duncan town. I remembered that every single establishment was lively and jumping with music, singing, and dancing. The drinks were flowing, and everyone seemed to be having a great time.

Thinking back, I further recalled that back in the day, gaining underage access to these bars was so easy. Most of us had fake IDs, but the bars really didn't care. They never even asked for proof of age. Bar owners were in it for one reason and one reason only. That was to make money. In a college town full of young, irresponsible adults, we were their money-making dream. What a dangerous racket. If I had only known then, what I know now.

For whatever reason, a reason I couldn't even remember, we had gotten into a disagreement. As I recollected, it was more like a heated argument ... alcohol induced, I'm sure. The night had pretty much ended, and it ended poorly. The bars were closing, which is when I stormed out in a frenzy.

I looked at Colin and said, "This was the last time I saw you, Colin. I have regretted my decision to walk out that door ever since."

I continued explaining that I had started walking. With no other way to get home, I continued to walk. In hindsight, it may not have been the smartest thing to do that night. That was to walk home in the dark alone, but back then, the streets were relatively safe. Or so we thought. In my rage and under the influence of alcohol, I marched onward. I was intent on getting home and into my nice warm bed.

Shortly after I began walking, I had the inclination to hitch a ride home. Hitchhiking was as normal as riding a bike back then. We did it all the time and knew mostly everyone who picked us up. Those we didn't know knew our parents or a sibling or neighbor. Being from a small town had its advantages. Everyone knew mostly everyone. But on this particular night, as I thought about stepping out to the road in an attempt to get a free ride, a feeling of dread came over me. It was a feeling I had never experienced before. Why was I all of a sudden afraid to do something that my friends and I were accustomed to doing all the time? The feeling was incredibly intense, so I heeded the warning and continued to walk.

122

A short while later, I revisited the idea to hitch a ride. As I started heading for the curb, I again had that feeling of dread. I couldn't explain it, but it was an awful feeling. It was as if a tiny little voice inside me was saying, "Don't do it." So, I heeded the warning for a second time.

After about a half hour of walking, I happened to turn and look behind me. I had just passed the entrance to the college when I saw a car exiting and turning in my direction. I had another hour to walk. It was late, and my feet were sore. I thought to myself, "This car may be the last chance I have to catch a ride home." In the spur of the moment, I pushed my reservations aside. I stepped to the curb, extended my right arm, and pointed my thumb toward the sky. The vehicle pulled over in front of me.

I approached the vehicle. It was a dark-colored, older model with four doors. I remember that it looked boxy. The windows were unusually dark, and I couldn't see inside very well. I opened the passenger-side door and hopped in. Immediately, a sense of doom and gloom came over me. It was the same awful feeling I had been experiencing since I started walking home. The man driving pulled away from the curb. Pushing the feeling aside, I greeted him as I normally would. "Hello," I said. "I'm just going straight down Central to Seventh Street."

In a normal situation, I would have told the driver to take me directly to the corner of my street. But this time felt different. And when the man did not respond to my greeting, it was unnerving. He merely looked straight ahead, with both hands gripping the wheel. I stared in dismay, studying his features through the muted glow of the interior lighting of the car. Although it was dark, he seemed to me to be of Spanish or Italian descent. He had long, dark, scraggly hair that sat in a disheveled heap upon his shoulders. He seemed to be of average build, although definitely much larger than my petite frame. It was difficult to tell how tall he was, but of one thing I was certain: he had to have been at least 20-30 years my senior. His scruffy facial hair only added to the perception that he was 'dirty'.

In absence of his response, I felt nervous. That nervousness was well placed because after a few minutes of driving, he began to slow down. Turning on his left blinker, he made a left-hand turn. In my mind, I freaked! With fear rising up within me, I tried to inconspicuously feel along the right side of my body for the door handle. I was sure that I had just indicated that I was going *straight* down Central Avenue to Seventh Street. These directions would have amounted to his driving about two more miles **straight** down the road, but instead, he turned. I began to question what I had or had not just told him. It is a natural reaction to start questioning yourself when the mind is trying to process the danger of a scenario playing out before your eyes. Most decent human beings do not immediately comprehend that another human being wants to harm them because they, themselves, do not think that way. The silence in that car was deafening. He still spoke not a word.

The particular road we were on was rather remote. It connected two main roads and extended the length of about one mile. Along one side was brush and fencing that separated the road from a highway above. The right was lined with fencing as well, but beyond that were a number of abandoned barns. This particular location was used once per year for the local county fair. There were no streetlights lining the road ... the darkness was desolate and cold. The road itself was ill-maintained and completely filled with potholes.

As I soaked in my surroundings, I observed that I was sitting on a bench seat. Like the back seat of a car is often one large, single seat, so was the front of his. This was a common feature on the more vintage-style vehicles. As we drove, he spoke for the first time.

He patted the leather seat next to him and said, "Come sit over here. I want to whisper in your ear."

"What?" I exclaimed, as if I hadn't registered what he had said.

This was the point at which I no longer questioned what was going on. I knew, beyond a shadow of a doubt, that this man had ill intentions. I knew I was in a really bad situation.

125

He patted the seat again and said, "Come sit over here. I want to whisper in your ear."

I instinctively mumbled some crazy answer as to why I couldn't slide closer.

He said, "Really?" and began to pull the car over to the side of the road.

As I felt the vehicle slow down, I grabbed the handle to the door. I tried to open it … I wanted to jump out … but …

It was locked!

It wouldn't open!

There was no way out!

I entered panic mode. This was when I first saw the knife. Wielding it in front of my face, his instructions were very clear. "Be quiet and do as I say, or I WILL kill you."

He said this with such conviction that I believed he would. I sat still and silent, not knowing what my next move would be … or if I even had a next move. And then the car came to a halt … a dead stop!

Brandishing a knife in one hand, he grabbed my wrist with the other. The bench seat style of the vehicle allowed him to easily drag me from the passenger side, out the driver's side door, and onto the pavement. Completely off balance, I stumbled to my feet as he continued to yank at me. Pulling me around to the back of the vehicle, he thrust me against the hood of the trunk. Bending me forward at the waist, he pushed up against me, grinding his pelvis into the back of my hips.

In one motion, a hand covered my mouth with some sort of cloth, while the other arm wrapped around the front of my body. Almost instantly I felt as though my body had gone limp as my head fell, lifeless, on top of the vehicle.

I'm not sure how long I had been unconscious, but when I opened my eyes, there he was … on top of me. It was apparent that I was no longer on the vehicle but rather on my back. In a state of delirium, it looked like I was surrounded by tall blades of grass, and with my dress pushed up around my neck, his body was moving up and down in a rough and rhythmic motion. I realized, he was inside me. I tried to scream, but his hand immediately pressed against my lips … almost smothering my ability to breathe. With the weight of his body pinning me down, he flashed the knife before my eyes and reminded me to comply. In defiance, I flailed my arms and squirmed under the heaviness of his skin.

Pressing the blade firmly under my chin, he declared, "Stop! Or I'll slit your throat. I mean it! I will kill you right here and now!"

His deep, raspy voice sent a shiver down my spine as he continued to beat his pelvis into mine. My body went limp, and I lay completely still, in total and unrelenting submission.

I could feel the pain searing from my abdomen all the way down through the length of my legs as he continued to beat against my flesh. Tears filled my eyes, and the more I cried, the harder he thrust into me. I pleaded for him to stop. With every plea, his dark, cold eyes penetrated deeper into mine. I will NEVER forget those eyes ... not for as long as I live. I squeezed mine closed and prayed for it to end.

Groaning a disgusting sound and completely out of breath, he pulled himself off of me. When he did, he lost his knife. As he was reaching to grasp for it in the weeds next to him, I knew, "This was my chance. It may be my only chance."

I began thrashing and kicking in violent protest to get away. By the grace of God, I managed to get to my feet and, without hesitation, began to run. I ran in the direction we had come from. It was the opposite direction that the car was facing. I didn't stop to look back to see if he was following me. I didn't stop running. My only thought was that I knew I had to get back to the main road.

In looking back, I recalled how difficult it should have been for me to get down that road. I remembered that I had worn retro wooden clogs that night. That particular stretch of road was always filled with massive potholes. Combined with the sheer darkness of the night, I long wondered how I had made it down that road with those shoes on and without faltering in my steps.

The rest of the way home was one big blur. I hid behind bushes and trees. With every pass of his car, I hid in the shadows. I knew that if he found me, I would surely be dead. I felt that was his intention all along. I was scared to death ... the entire way. Would he plant himself in the trees somewhere along the way? Maybe jump out at me from behind a car? Or, pull me in as I passed a row of hedges?

That feeling of doom had returned. I knew that the closer I got to my original drop-off point, he would surely be waiting ... somewhere. I didn't hesitate to listen to that voice this time. I heeded the warning and took a dreaded shortcut, over the railroad tracks and through the backyards. I feared the darkness of the brush that lined the tracks, the dilapidated old abandoned depot building, and the hobos that frequented the area. The thought of having to pass through this remote area alone at night was terrifying in itself. But I knew the alternative was far worse. Ultimately, though, it would serve as the shortcut that would help me find my way home ... and save my life.

I flung open the back door and collapsed on the floor in the back shed. The house was dark and still. Everyone was asleep. Should I wake my mother up and confide in her embrace, where I might feel safe again? No … I was afraid. I was afraid that she and my father would be angered by my late arrival. There were still rules I was expected to abide by. Instead, my immediate response was to jump in a hot shower. I had been violently and irreparably assaulted. The dirt and filth permeated to my bones. All I wanted to do was to feel clean again. But it didn't matter how much I scrubbed; that soiled feeling would remain for many years to come.

I felt a whole mix of emotions that night. I was only nineteen. I felt so alone. Cowering in the base of the shower, as the water dripped down my cheeks, all I could do was curl up into a ball and cry.

CHAPTER 14

Angel's Whisper

Saturday, July 20, 2024

Colin looked at me with tear-filled eyes, "But Sonny. You weren't alone. You were never alone. I would have been there for you."

I shook my head back and forth. "I was still a kid, Colin. In an adult body, albeit. But in my mind, I was still a kid."

I explained that being nineteen years old, I was still immature. When something like that happens to you, it changes you. In an instant, you are a different person. And you can't get back the person you were. Not ever! From that moment on, I had changed. I was a different person than he knew.

"I made so many mistakes, Colin. First, I made the mistake of not telling my mother. I have been haunted with the thought that this maniac may have gone on to violate other girls ... and even kill them. To this day, I still have not told her. I made the mistake of taking a shower. I washed away any hope of ever bringing my perpetrator to justice. I made the mistake of blaming myself for hitchhiking in the first place; I'd convinced myself that somehow, I deserved what I got. I made the mistake of running away from you that night. While leaving Duncan set the stage for many wonderful things in my life, namely my children, it tore me away from my one true love. It took many years before I allowed myself to face the emotions from that attack. I'm not sure that I will ever fully heal."

I explained to Colin that one of the emotions that consumed my every thought was that of guilt. I felt so guilty that I had gotten into that man's car that night. A large part of me had convinced myself that I had asked for it by voluntarily putting myself out on the road for his taking. I was hard on myself; I was my own worst enemy. I had so many warnings that I ultimately chose not to heed. And it was all to my own detriment. I couldn't comprehend how I had been so stupid.

"Because he had raped me, I couldn't face you," I told him. "Because I felt responsible for what had happened, it was my fault that another man, a disgustingly vile man, had violated me. I didn't think that was something you could ever forgive me for. It was easier for me to run."

132

I continued, "And I soon would learn that the one thing I could never outrun was self-forgiveness. I would eventually realize that all I was running from was myself."

I continued to share my innermost feelings about how dirty that night had made me feel. It took many years before I felt I could wash away the filth. This led to a huge lack of self-worth and allowed me to accept things I should have never accepted. Mainly, my marriage. Although, I did get my boys from that union. That is something I would never, ever regret.

I explained that for a time, I was even angry with him ... him, meaning Colin. I was angry about our fight. "If we had not gotten into the fight that night, I wouldn't have been walking home ... alone ... in the dark."

I continued, "For years I had tormented myself wondering why you never followed me. Why didn't you come to save me? You were my knight in shining armor—you were supposed to rescue me."

With those words, I broke down into a slobbering heap.

Colin reached out and wrapped both of his strong and loving arms around me.

"I'm so sorry, Sonny. I am so sorry for everything. I'm sorry for that fight. I'm sorry you had to experience this horror. And I'm sorry you have carried this burden all alone for all these years."

"Most of all, Sonny, I'm sorry I didn't come to save you."

As I sat sobbing in his embrace, I buried my face deep within his chest. He was trying to remain strong for me, even though I knew he was shedding a tear or two. I knew that no one was at fault. No one except my assailant. Most of all, I knew it wasn't Colin's fault. It was my choice to leave the bar that night. It was my choice to leave alone. It was my choice to hitchhike and my choice to accept that ride. All my own choices.

I felt as if I had opened up a water spigot. Having pent up the truth for so many years, it all came gushing out at a turn of the handle. A sense of relief washed over me, and I felt as if a weight had been lifted off my shoulders. This was the first time I had *ever* shared my secret.

But still, I knew there was more. The rest would have to wait for another day.

I pulled my head back and confessed, "In an effort to run as far away as I could get, as quickly as I could get there, I enlisted in the military. It literally took me one week from the time I entered the recruitment office until the day I boarded the bus and left home for the next twenty years. I went in as an enlisted recruit with no assigned job. The rest was sheer fate.

Colin looked at me with profound understanding and compassion. "I'm still here for you, Sonny. This does not change how I have always felt about you. If anything, it only makes me admire you more."

In an effort to fill in the gaps, I explained that I found myself working within the intelligence field when I first entered the military. My daughter came early in my career, as did my marriage. I continued my education, and after a couple of years, I had finished my degree and earned my Bachelor of Science in Criminal Justice. A short time later, I was accepted into Officer Training School and transitioned to the role of Commissioned Officer. I spent the next five years assigned to their Office of Special Investigations, focusing on felony crimes such as murder, rape, assault, trafficking, sex crimes, black market activities, and other serious crimes. During those five years I completed a dual master's program in forensics and psychology. That led me to my current employer, where I have spent the past twelve years. The last eight have been as a criminal profiler. It was the early stage of my career as a criminal profiler that ultimately led to the breakup of my marriage.

I explained to Colin that in my best attempt to bury the horrific memories of that night, I immersed myself in school, work, and family. Staying busy 24/7 was how I survived. The events of that evening influenced every aspect of my life ... from my career choices to my decision to marry and, ultimately, to remain in the façade of a loveless marriage.

The night of the attack had become my drive. It's been my motivation. For the past twenty years, I have made a conscious decision to hunt down as many of these psychologically deranged individuals as I could. I've wanted nothing more than to lock them away where they can no longer be a threat to society and hurt girls like me. And I've been pretty successful so far. I tell myself that maybe I had to go through the experiences I have gone through in order to be able to understand and help others.

"As sick as it may sound, Colin, it has even been my secret hope to come face-to-face with my own assailant someday." I continued, "Because the next time, it would be different."

"The next time ...

... I would be strong!

... I would be in control!

... I would *not* be afraid!

... And I would *not* run away!"

Colin looked at me intensely. "And *that* passion is what makes you so good at what you do!"

I returned the intensity of his gaze and smiled. I appreciated his compliment, but I knew that where there was success, there was also failure. And in this particular instance, I felt like I had failed. I felt like I had failed both Anna and the Pennsylvania victim. Had I been able to do something more to stop this maniac after the Ohio murder, their lives would have been spared.

Trying not to be a total Debbie Downer, I acknowledged his kind words. I explained, however, that while my passion has played a role, so also have the various teams of professionals that have surrounded me. And I'd be remiss if I failed to acknowledge that God-given guidance that seems to always lead me in the right direction.

I explained that that night had been a pivotal moment in my life where I had learned to listen to the voice within me ... the gut feelings ... my angel's whisper. Whatever it was, its presence was undeniable for me, and it had continued to guide me throughout my career ... throughout my entire life, for that matter.

Surprisingly, Colin did not flinch. I was sure that the mere mention of this spiritual aspect of my experience would catch him off guard. Maybe it would even shy him away. But he got it. He got me. And all was good in our world.

As luck would have it, we spent the rest of the evening and the next day together. In delightful conversation, both in and out of the bedroom, it was as if we had never been apart. We couldn't get enough of one another. I felt as if by sharing my secret, we were brought closer together. What an irony, since I had lived my life thinking it would do the exact opposite.

Our little fantasy world, however, would be short-lived. Monday morning would find us driving to Ackerton, Pennsylvania, and meeting the investigative team that Chief Jeremy had put together. We would spend the afternoon in meetings and setting up what would become known as the *War Room*. This is where we would share and analyze every detail we uncovered and dissect every piece of evidence or lead. It would mark the beginning of what would become many long days and sleepless nights. But I welcomed this opportunity to do my part in putting this psychopathic killer out of business.

I was feeling both anxious and optimistic about this investigation. I wanted to get it started, and I wanted to get it done. I had a good feeling. I was determined that tomorrow would be filled with both promise and hope… the promise of being one day closer to removing another wrong in this world, and the hope that we might make this world a safer place …

… one day at a time.

CHAPTER 15

Modus Operandi

Monday, July 22, 2024

The first ray of sunlight lit up the room as I slid into the dining room chair. The irresistible, yeasty scent of cinnamon buns lingered in the air. Mom had spent the morning whipping up a fresh batch, and she did not skimp on the sweetness of the cinnamon sugar or the melt-in-your-mouth cream cheese drizzle. The gooey goodness brought with it a sense of comfort and contentment. Washing it down with a sip of freshly brewed coffee and staring out the window, a smile widened across my face. I was looking forward to this morning's chat with Mom before I set off for work.

It had been a week since *The Daily Disturber* had named Fred as the key suspect in Anna's murder. The local chatter was starting to die down, but soon, now, the public would know that we were actually looking for a serial killer. I squeezed my eyes closed and clenched my lips. Taking in a deep breath and releasing a slow and steady sigh, I shook my head from side to side. I shuddered to think of what the next headline might read. This is a perfect example of why I have always despised the media. It doesn't matter who they exploit, as long as it can help them to increase their readership and make a profit. This little local paper had a reputation of thriving on tactics of 'shock and awe'. But they needed to be careful with this one. Our community was going to be terrified, and for this story, they needed to act more like a reputable newspaper and less like a gossip tabloid.

"Good morning, Mom," I greeted my mother as she entered the room.

"Good morning, Sonny," she said with a bright and cheery smile.

A welcome break from my thoughts; we haven't had much time to visit these last few days. But I had news I thought she'd enjoy hearing. I shared with her that I had spoken with my ex-husband. He had agreed to send the twins on a plane to visit for two weeks before they started back at school. Although the time would be short-lived, this was a welcome and unexpected visit, and I was happy to have them at all.

Joyously rising to her feet, she exclaimed, "Jackson and Jayce? I haven't seen them since I came to visit you when they were babies!" Smiling from ear to ear, she continued, "And what about Josie? Will she come too?"

I replied, "I spoke to Josie this morning, and yes, she is going to come too. It may only be for a couple weeks as well because she will be starting college. She's so excited to see you!" I gave Mom a huge grin.

I was excited too. I hadn't seen them in over three weeks, and their absence was wearing on my heart. Phone calls just can't replace warm, real-life cuddles and hugs from your littles ... even your littles who are all grown up. The more I thought about their visit, the more I was looking forward to sharing with them this pretty little community where I grew up. It almost made me question why it had taken me so long to come back.

In the back of my mind I wondered, though, how Colin would feel about meeting them. This was a definite deal breaker. No matter what I felt for Colin or how good we were together, his acceptance of my children was requisite for any relationship we might have. I planned to discuss their visit with him after today's meeting.

Arriving in Ackerton, Chief Jeremy greeted me at the door and accompanied me to the conference room. Walking down the short hallway, I could hear the chatter emanating from the room we were about to enter. There, he introduced me to the other key players on the team. In addition to Chief Jeremy as team lead, Colin as lead investigator, and myself as the criminal profiler, there would be two other investigators representing the Pennsylvania and Ohio cases, a trace evidence examiner, a criminalist, a technology expert, and several support staff providing data analysis and administrative assistance. All members of the team possessed outstanding credentials, and I was very confident in our ability to work together.

Following several briefings regarding details about each of the individual cases, Colin had presented new evidence from Anna's final autopsy. The evidence confirmed that the assailant was, unquestionably, a biological male. As was the case in the other attacks, no signs of ejaculation were found. With Anna, however, previously pending forensics testing confirmed the retrieval of epithelial cells. The results of these cells would identify the attacker's biological sex. This was a formality that would serve to corroborate an important detail about our suspect. It would also serve as important DNA evidence to tie the attacker to her murder. In the absence of DNA, the autopsies of the other two victims had not definitively confirmed our attacker as a male. The similarity of their internal injuries, along with the list of other irrefutable likenesses, however, connected them to the same individual.

Our perp had made *a vital* mistake. Our team was well underway, scouring criminal history records in an attempt to match his DNA. I knew it was just a matter of time.

It was my turn to brief the group. I had managed to formulate a lengthy and detailed accounting of the type of individual we were looking for. All eyes were on me as I shared with them the suspect profile.

"Our suspect is a man of many complexities. He has a job or hobby that requires travel. At minimum, he travels along the Lake Erie shoreline. We cannot eliminate, however, the possibility that he serves an area throughout the East Coast or beyond. He is somehow affiliated with the swimming industry. He may be a coach or a recruiter of some sort, since he targets women associated with universities. Maybe he even presents himself as a like-minded athlete. He also has something to do with either the pharmaceutical industry or institutions of higher education, mainly research colleges, where they develop and research the paralytic drug, vecuronium, used to incapacitate his victims. Our perp has a connection with one, or the other, or both. His knowledge of the sport of swimming would suggest that he may have been an accomplished swimmer at one time.

He likes to be in complete control. His use of a paralytic drug allows him to maintain control of his victims at all times. While some criminals are aroused by the combative behavior of their victims, our perp is aroused by their submission. This is marked by their inability to move or rebel. He may also be using the drug to maintain consciousness as a way of convincing himself that his victims are willing partners. He can see the fear in their eyes. This turns him on. It is also possible that he may have a physical disability or limitation that prevents him from physically overpowering his

143

victims. It may even be his size and stature, which would indicate another reason why he needs to incapacitate them.

Our perp is motivated by thrill. He is a thrill seeker who loves the rush of adrenaline. He has likely had significant exposure to terrifying situations. We are looking for someone whose childhood was filled with sexually exploitative experiences. Normal people experience an adrenaline rush similar to a primitive fight or flight response when they are threatened. Our perp, however, goes to a whole new level and experiences a biological response that results in intense sexual arousal. The bigger the rush, the bigger the climax. I believe at one time he was highly involved in thrill-seeking activities, which likely quelled his temptations. However, for some reason, he was unable to continue to pursue those activities ... maybe due to an injury or accident. As a result, he resorts back to what is common and familiar to him in order to achieve that high.

Additionally, he may be trying to recreate these fear-to-climax experiences for his victims. This could be his internal justification for his actions—to bring pleasure to others. This concept is more about him, though, than 'caring' about his victims since he has a psychopathic personality and grandiose view of himself. More likely, seeing the terror in their eyes triggers the adrenaline rush that he keeps coming back for. While he may be somewhat physically limited, he is someone who enjoys rough and uninhibited sex, as is demonstrated by the internal injuries sustained by the victims. He likely has a fetish for kinky clubs, websites, or other atmospheres where he can exchange ideas with like-minded individuals. Based on his behaviors and inclinations, I would suggest a past riddled with sexual exploitation, and our perp was the star victim.

Our man WANTS us to know that these cases are all related. Although he kills in a remote location, it is a location that he is pretty assured of having his victims found within 24 hours of their death. He is a meticulous and detailed planner, likely carefully selecting and stalking his victims beforehand. He is an average "Joe," comfortably melding into society. Enough so that his victims trust him. Although he may have been athletic at one time, I believe he was less than popular among the girls. Maybe he wasn't very good looking. Compounded by a disability of some sort, he was left with an even more bruised self-image, feeling that he lacks desirability by the opposite sex.

Finally, he purposefully plants a red ribbon on each victim by tying it around their necks; he ties it with a left-handed bow. He does this after he uses it to strangle them. He's marking his prey; he is proud of his conquests, and he wants us to know. That is **his** mark. But why a red ribbon? What does it mean? We should keep that in mind as this investigation progresses.

I believe also that he has returned to the scene of each crime. Maybe he's even interacted with law enforcement. It's like a game of cat and mouse to him. Like dangling catnip to see if the cat will bite, he's toying with us. He is pompous enough to believe that we will never catch him. And THAT, my friends, is why we will."

At this point, I took a variety of questions from the team. Many interesting queries were addressed, and just as intriguing were the different perspectives. It was refreshing to gather new ideas and realize the uniform commitment among the team members.

As a final reminder, I wanted to impart this thought. I wanted to reiterate that we were not dealing with your average psychopath. Not every psychopath is an evil person. Ours, however, had obviously risen to a more dangerous level based on his criminal behavior. He was, for certain, an evil person. He clearly lacked empathy, he was a liar and a manipulator, and he was likely deprived of remorse. In addition to those traditional characteristics of a psychopathic personality, he also exhibited symptoms of Antisocial Personality Disorder (ASPD). As a result, he held a complete disregard for social norms and ill regard for other people's rights. Likely suffering from dual conditions, he was a very dangerous man.

After a brief break, we reassembled to consider a synopsis of the victims. I continued,

"Our perpetrator selects his victims based upon availability, vulnerability, and desirability. We know that the victims are all female, fair-skinned, and of European descent. They were all attractive with long, dark hair. Each was of similar size and stature, all being of petite build. All were swimmers, and as such, all had a broader build to their shoulders, and all were physically appealing. All had some kind of connection to a university swimming pool facility. What doesn't match up is that the victim from the most recent killing in Duncan, New York, was much older than the other two. She was not a college student, as was the case with the other two. However, she did attend open swim sessions at a local university to train for a triathlon. Based on evidence, we believe our Duncan, NY, victim was lured to a remote beach along Lake Erie, where her body was found. Due to the close correlation between these cases, it is believed that the other two victims were lured as well. All had taken a fresh swim in the lake water before their death. We don't believe they were at their final resting spot by chance.

All three victims died from ligature strangulation. Thus, the red ribbon was tied around each of the victim's necks. All presented with fractured hyoid bones, which is typically associated with strangulation. All three were positioned in a similar fashion, lying on their backs, and were partially clad. All had been sexually assaulted. All women sustained similar genital injuries of varying degrees. None displayed defensive wounds. A small needle prick was found on the right leg of the last victim. Forensics revealed vecuronium, a paralytic agent, in her system, which would explain the lack of defensive wounds; again, a probable scenario for the previous two victims as well. It is likely that our perp is left-handed, having used his dominant hand to puncture the victim. It is presumed that the dominant left hand was also used to tie all bows. Autopsy findings should be reviewed for the first two victims; we should be looking for anything that might potentially identify an injection site. We needed to review all photos, descriptions, and notes that might be available. Forensics should re-test available DNA of the other two victims, specifically for the presence of vecuronium or other, similar paralytic drugs."

I explained that in addition to these three cases, there were two more cases that came to my attention during my initial analysis of these events. They reflected similar victim scenarios; one occurred in Ohio and the other in Pennsylvania. Both were worthy of our review and consideration of possessing a connection to this case. In addition, I suggested that the team expand their search and research any unsolved cases around Lake Erie within the past ten years or so, ones that may mimic our current cases. I suggested that this could be even larger than we had initially anticipated. I indicated that while reviewing any new cases, we needed to keep two things in mind ... the perpetrator's modus operandi and his signature.

The Modus Operandi is his "mode of operating", also known as his M.O. It consists of the techniques, behavior, and habits used in the course of committing his crimes. These are learned behaviors, and as the criminal gains experience and confidence, his M.O. will likely evolve to meet the needs of the crime. In our current case, our perp's M.O. consists of how he gains access to his victims, the particular days and times of day he chooses for each attack, and the weapons and tools he uses. It would also include the methods he uses to cultivate trust, how he lures his victims, and the type of locations he selects. Although we know many of the details already, there is still so much more to be learned.

His signature involves those behaviors that serve his emotional needs. These will remain constant among the various crimes. If there is any deviation, it will likely be the result of variations that occur as his crimes progress over time. In this particular case, our perp leaves his signature red ribbon tied in a bow around each of the victim's necks. His signature also includes the ritualistic nature of these attacks.

I cautioned them, however, to remain open to new and evolving events. An older case may appear to be similar, yet may be missing a certain common element that we are seeing in the current cases. In these situations, the cases in question should not be readily dismissed since the perp's M.O. or signature may have evolved over time.

We truly had no idea how deep down the rabbit hole we were about to go.

As the day progressed, each of the team members settled into their designated work areas. Colin and I managed to steal a sensual glance or two from across the room; we even shared a hidden touch or two as we brushed up against each other in the hallway. Mostly, however, we were able to maintain our composure and remain fully engaged in the events and developments of the day without any major distraction. While I was proud of our shared professionalism, I was also grateful for those few stolen moments that broke up the day. Welcome diversions, they were both alluring and enticing.

As the day was coming to an end, Colin and I caught a glimpse of one another. Each of us smiled. We could no longer deny the growing sexual tension between us. That would explain why, by the time we arrived back at his house, the provocation had reached its peak. We hadn't even made it to the front door before we found ourselves in each other's arms. Soon we lay breathlessly naked atop the soft blades of grass that enveloped us.

How is it that amongst all this doom and gloom and chaos, I would finally find my way back home?

CHAPTER 16

The Perfect Night

This day couldn't have come soon enough. The boy's flight would be landing at 10:02 a.m. It was a bright, sunny morning with an expected high of eighty-six degrees Fahrenheit. With no clouds in the sky, we entered the terminal where we would soon greet the boys upon their arrival. I was excited for Colin to meet them, so I was glad that he had agreed to join me. I know he was excited too, but I could sense his nervousness as he anxiously paced back and forth across the floor. I reached out to him and grabbed his hand.

Reassuringly, I said, "Don't worry. They're going to love you."

Colin forced a smile and gave me a nod. I smiled back, thinking that deep down inside, I knew I was right. Even so, there was still that little piece inside me that was fearful they might not. He squeezed my hand as if he knew what I was thinking, and as he did, his soft yet firm touch reassured **me** that all would be just fine.

And it **was** just fine. As I stared enthusiastically at the gate, there appeared two adorably handsome, blonde-haired, blue-eyed boys, each holding onto an arm of a lovely young stewardess. Both appeared to be chatting away without a care in the world until they got a glimpse of me.

"Mom!" they yelled in unison, as they both came rushing to give me a long, overdue hug.

No matter how old my boys were, they would always need their mom. And, she would always need them. I smiled to myself. What a warm feeling it was to finally have them here with me.

After the initial emotions of their arrival waned, I placed my hands on each of their shoulders, and without saying a word, I glanced over at Colin. The boys looked at me and then at Colin and back at me. Together, they began to smile.

"Boys," I said. "This is my friend, Colin."

Colin greeted each of them with a firm handshake and a warm, friendly grin. As he shook each of their hands, he said, "A firm handshake is a sign of good friendship."

To the boys, at their youthful age, I doubt they understood the magnitude of Colin's gesture. But I knew exactly what he meant. I knew enough about Colin to know that when he extended his hand in friendship, he was extending it as a friend for life. That gesture bore a lot of meaning for him, and for me, it was yet another affirmation that all would be well.

The hour ride home seemed like it took forever. The boys were so excited to experience new people and a new place. At eight years old, their inquiring minds wanted to know anything about everything. Colin drove the scenic route along the shoreline of Lake Erie instead of taking the highway. There was one question, followed by another question, followed by even more questions. The peak of their curiosity, however, was not about the new scenery. It was about Colin. They asked all about who he was and how he knew me. He actually did quite well in response to their inquisition. I guess that comes naturally after dealing with the public for so many years. I was surprised, though, when out of Jayce's mouth came the words ...

"Are you my mom's boyfriend?"

He was looking in Colin's direction, and I hadn't quite anticipated that he would just blurt it out like that. Instinctively, I began to gag on the muffin I was nibbling. As I cleared my throat, I exclaimed, "Jayce!"

In his boldness, he giggled at my reaction and shared a side eye with his brother. Both were quite amused.

"Well, I guess that's what you could call me." Colin imparted an endearing smile as he nodded in agreement.

I looked at him inquisitively and a little amused, since we hadn't formally discussed our status. But I was happily content with his response and smiled too. Jayce and Jackson both seemed excited at the prospect that Mom had a new boyfriend. I was relieved. They really hadn't seen me with a male friend before. Sure, I went on dates, but none that I had introduced them to. So, this was something new, and I was really glad that they were accepting of it.

The biggest test, however, would be how Josie would respond. I had shared snippets of mine and Colin's courtship with her, and she seemed genuinely excited for me. But I wasn't sure how well she would embrace the reality of me having a man in my life when it was right before her eyes. We were all charting new territory, and I was so appreciative of Colin's patience. I know it couldn't have been an easy experience for him either, but he was all in, so he said. The big reveal with Josie would take place this evening over family dinner.

Arriving in Duncan was bound to be a cultural shock for Jayce and Jackson. The boys had traveled before, but they had never been introduced to such a small rural community like the one I grew up in. Hearing about it and experiencing it were two very different things.

As we approached my old homestead, the boys caught the visual of my mother's large two-story home with its red brick-colored, wood-shingle siding and similarly shingled roof. It must have looked primitive compared to the modern designs they were accustomed to. They were used to growing up in newer developments with modern modular homes, complete with community swimming pools and other amenities. But this area was different. It was an old town steeped in centuries-old history. My mom's 150-year-old, well-kept middle-class home was not unlike the others that stood tall along this mature tree-lined street. The enclosed front porch was enhanced by three walls of windows, dressed in old venetian blinds that were drawn open wide. Busy voices bustled about this quaint, friendly street. "Hello! Good-bye!" A cheerful eye ... all lent to the daily demeanor. This was a completely different atmosphere for them. This place that I had long ago viewed as a safe little haven was the place I called *home.* I was eager to share it with them.

The boys were in awe as we pulled into the driveway. Especially when the first glimpse of their grandmother, frantically barreling out the back door, was evident. It was an almost comical sight to see this little old Polish lady moving as quickly as she was ... her tattered black loafers moving one foot in front of the other at lightning pace. Just as entertaining was her sweet little apron she wore to protect her light green floral print

155

dress. I knew she wanted to look presentable for meeting the boys and hadn't expected to be cooking when we first drove up.

Mom was so ecstatic to see how they'd grown from the little babes they once were that it didn't much matter at this point what her appearance was. With tears in her eyes, she knelt to the ground, arms wide open. The look on her face was a combination of latent heartache and pure joy. It made me realize that through all these years, I never stopped to consider the depth of my mother's own feelings. How she must have felt in my absence … after all this time. With no explanation, she has never asked questions; she simply trusted my decisions. I know how it felt not seeing my own children for a little over two weeks. That can't even begin to compare to how she has felt for all those years of missing her own daughter. And now, after eight years, she gets to meet her twin grandsons for the second time and gets to know them for the first. My heart felt heavy knowing that I was responsible for the burden she had carried, but I knew I could never tell her the truth. The truth about why I had left.

I watched Mom whisk them into her gentle and loving arms. I remembered that embrace well and knew again that all would be just fine.

As Mom shuffled the boys off to show them their bedroom, Colin and I retreated to the living room. I reclined back into my favorite chair, laid my head back, and closed my eyes. My thoughts drifted to Anna… then to the investigation.

Over the past couple weeks, Chief Jeremy had successfully enlisted the services of a single forensics lab where the process for ensuring consistency of testing had begun. Our team had been busy pursuing various leads. Investigators were working to identify pharmaceutical companies and universities that may be involved in the development or research of paralytic drugs. They were searching for trucking companies with eastern routes, particularly along the Lake Erie trail. They were trying to identify other job types that might require frequent travel. They were investigating clubs or gathering rooms, both online and off, that might cater to kinky or even sadistic sexual experiences. They had begun their research of East Coast university campus programs with a heavy focus on competitive swim; they were hoping to identify special programs, camps, or recruitment activities that might be used to lure potential victims. Phone records, crime scene photos, webcams, witnesses, interviews … my mind swirled around the immensity of the case. For me, this investigation actually started with the initial Ohio case three years prior. I was hopeful that with new evidence, Anna's murder would be the last and we could bring it all to closure.

"And what about Fred and Emily?" I thought.

I knew they were in the clear, but there was that tiny little part of me that still questioned their connection. My gut was telling me that this was the work of a male assailant acting alone, while my training taught me to never overlook the obvious. At least with Anna's death, one had motive and the other had opportunity. That was obvious. Yet, there was nothing that physically connected them to any of the cases. I felt bad that I had to think of them, mostly Emily, in this way. Unfortunately, I have found that too many times, the answers being sought are right under our noses. For this reason alone, I will never fully erase anyone from my list of potentials until the case is fully solved.

Reverting my thoughts back to the boys, I knew that the next couple weeks would be a delicate balance between my children and my work. But for now, it was Sunday. A day of rest. A day to relish in family. And a day to enjoy life. Tomorrow would be here soon enough, and with it, just another day at the office ... or in my case, another day spent trying to dissect the mind of a psychopathic killer.

The day flew by. It is true that time flies when you are having fun. Before we knew it, though, Josie would be meeting us for dinner at The Lake House Inn. It was the perfect backdrop for all five of us to spend some quality time together in a sophisticated yet relaxed atmosphere. Seated on the outdoor patio, the restaurant was well known for its sunset views and expansive menu.

Colin and I, along with the boys, were the first to arrive. We were seated at the northernmost outdoor patio table, offering the best unobstructed beach view. There was a slight breeze whispering through the air as we were surrounded by the floral fragrance of climbing clematis. The vibrant colors sprawled delicately across the trellis that acted as a makeshift roof above our heads. The sun had begun its spectacular descent in marvelous shades of orange and yellow when Josie walked in. She looked in our direction, and as she headed toward us, she smiled from ear to ear.

My heart was full.

It was the beginning of what was to become the *perfect night!*

CHAPTER 17

A Blessing or A Curse

Monday, July29, 2024

The evening **had** been perfect. Perfect in every way, except for the way the clock ticked forward. Perfection never seems to last, and so neither did our exquisite night. Mom was happy to hear all about it, as she apologized once again for not being able to join us. I think she secretly planned it that way, though, so the kiddos could get to know Colin. I shared Josie's reaction to Colin and described how well they had hit it off. I even suggested that they had an instant connection, not much unlike Colin and me. Not in a romantic way, of course, but an unexplainable connection nonetheless.

"It was weird, in a really good way, how well they got along," I said.

Overall, it had all worked out well, and I hoped we could do it again while the kids were still in town.

As I took a swig of my coffee, I noticed the Monday morning newspaper folded next to me. Mom raised her brows and said, "Read the headline on the bottom of the front page."

Reaching for the paper, I carefully opened it up. I can't say I was surprised to see, in big, bold, black letters, **"Serial Killer Among Us!"**

"Ugh!" I sighed as I rolled my eyes back and slumped in my chair.

The media had finally regurgitated the details of the case to the public. Of course, they would exaggerate every detail, true and untrue, with the most magnificent theatrics. People would be scared. Everyone would begin to question who they could trust. People who once felt safe would now be locking their doors and bolting their windows. I knew how this worked. Especially in a small town where this type of thing was so foreign to them. They would become acutely aware of their surroundings, and it would quickly become the norm to constantly look over their shoulders. Neighbors would look at neighbors with intense, and sometimes irrational, distrust and suspicion. The line between normal fears, extreme anxiety, and profound paranoia would be blurred. The normally bustling streets would turn near empty at dusk, as people would retreat to the safety of

161

their homes. The Duncan Police Station would turn into a call center for tips—mostly baseless—until a suspect was in custody. How I hated to see this beautiful little town turn into a fear-mongering community where friends would begin to turn on friends.

It was imperative, now more than ever, for Colin to release as much information as he could in order to put the residents' minds at ease that they would not be the next victim. Maybe, moreover, to limit the blame game and avoid the ruin of friendships that were years in the making. How we handled, and even controlled, the media coverage was crucial in keeping the dynamics of this community intact. It was no surprise, then, when Colin called my cell phone to request that I join him at a meeting with the editor-in-chief.

"One hour," he said.

"I'll be there!" I replied as I laid down the paper.

"Don't worry about the kids," Mom said. "I've got big plans for us today. We'll stay busy and see you at dinner."

"Moms … They always make things better." I thought, as I smiled. "At least mine always did. Oh, how I wished I could go back in time and have known then what I know now." I leaned over and gave her a quick hug.

"Thanks, Mom." I knew they would be in good hands.

"One question," Mom said. "Do I need to be worried about this insane killer on the loose?"

"No," I replied. "He doesn't want you or the kids. Well actually, keep Josie away from the college campus. Just to be safe. Please."

"Consider it done!" Mom said. "I'll have her help me with the boys today. We'll be headed in the opposite direction from the campus. It'll give us a chance to catch up on lost time."

"Thanks again, Mom." It was one less thing for me to worry about for the day.

A couple hours later would find Colin and me nearing the Ackerton Police Station, where we would attend the weekly team briefing. Our meeting at *The Daily Disturber* had actually gone surprisingly well. As a side note, I really should call the newspaper by its formal name, *The Daily Wire*, but I have always known it by its nickname. Old habits die hard.

We all agreed to complete transparency with the case. We'd share as much as we possibly could without risking the integrity of the investigation. The Editor-in-Chief agreed that *The Daily Wire* would remain fact-based and present information in an unbiased manner. We had successfully convinced them that there would be no need for exaggerated details; their readership would benefit as a result of their exclusive access to local emerging details. We were all in agreement that preservation of our community was the main goal, while bringing them the most up-to-date and accurate details possible. We planned to hold similar meetings with the local newspapers in Pennsylvania and Ohio as well. They would be given exclusive content respective to their area, and in return, they would minimize the dramatization of the details; they would stick to the facts in the hopes of avoiding mass hysteria.

As we arrived at the Ackerton station, Chief Jeremy greeted Colin and me with what he felt was exciting news. The cell phone I had found at the Duncan, New York, crime scene had been unlocked. They positively identified that the phone had belonged to Anna. Our forensics team was able to view all the photos, text messages, and recent phone calls. Among the information they were able to retrieve, they had access to an exact route with times that she had traveled, thanks to an application she had installed on her phone. This was a key finding in confirming the timeline up to her death.

In addition, two important details had emerged. First was a whole group of selfie photos Anna had taken on her phone. In the background of several of the photos was a man dressed in dark clothing. We knew this would be the same man that was in Fred's photo as well as the man that Witness Valerie had suggested was present at the pool. The other detail, which was hugely important to the case, was a voice recording that Anna made. The beginning time stamp was 8:03 p.m., and the recording lasted about thirty minutes before the battery appears to have died. The sun set at 8:23 p.m. on the evening of her death. This was likely not a long time before she died.

Chief Jeremy indicated that the recording was of Anna and her potential killer. She must have sensed something wrong and purposefully planted her cell phone in the crevice of the rocks.

He explained that the contents were extremely graphic, and he warned me to review the written transcript and avoid listening to the actual recording. Considering my relationship with Anna, I knew that emotionally, sticking to the transcript was the logical thing to do. On the other hand, the professional side of me insisted on reliving every detail, as closely as I could, in order to get inside the suspect's head.

I knew that this was one of the biggest pieces of evidence we could have come across, and it literally fell into my lap. Normal protocol would have me listen to the tape had I not known the victim. Since I was fully convinced that it was Anna who led me to find it in the first place, the least I could do was to walk as closely as I could with her in death. It was my intent to review the contents of the phone before the end of the week. In particular, I would listen to the recording first, then likely follow up by reading the transcript to ensure I didn't miss anything.

As all the team members settled into the briefing room, our discussion would revolve around updates from the previous week and the direction our investigation would take in the coming week.

We began with an update from our technology expert, who had scoured Anna's laptop to follow up on rumors of online dating. Unfortunately, there was nothing to support that Anna had met anyone in the online community. This finding was consistent with both the Pennsylvania and Ohio victims.

Our attention was soon focused on updates from the criminalist. Otherwise known as a forensic scientist, the criminalist was more formally known as Doc Marvin. Doc would focus on the application of scientific methods to recognize, collect, identify, and compare physical evidence.

I knew Doc Marvin well and had recommended him for our team. Having worked with him a number of times in the past, he was recognized for his expertise in this area of forensics and was considered to be among the top in the nation. Although we didn't seem to have a whole lot of physical evidence, we were hopeful that with what we did have, an expert could piece together the breadcrumbs and corroborate emerging theories. Doc would be **that** piece of the puzzle. He would be primarily responsible for reconstructing the events of the crimes by evaluating the physical evidence and the crime scenes.

What we already knew ... in each case, the victims were met at a swimming facility located on a university campus. It didn't matter if it was a public or private university; it only mattered that it was an institution of higher ed. We were inclined to believe that this location of choice was based on the preferred age range of the intended victims as well as their love of swimming. Except for Anna. She didn't fit this theory. Anna may have shared the love of swimming, but she was definitely far more mature than the other two victims. A key point that needed further consideration.

Doc confirmed that there was enough videotape evidence to verify that our victims went voluntarily from the universities to the locations where their bodies were found. He had reviewed countless clips that were collected during all three investigations. An interesting observation was that in each case, the perp led the way while the victims followed. This served to confirm my early thoughts that Anna had been lured to her final resting place, the place at the lake where she would take her last breath.

Doc then went one step further and questioned whether we had thought to seek out video evidence that might trace the route of the offender **prior** to arriving at the university. Chief Jeremy explained that we had, but the trail quickly went cold on a public roadway that branched out through the countryside.

On the flip side, however, while leaving the scene of the crime, law enforcement had been able to track the suspect's movement to a little dive motel near the lake, close to the Pennsylvania state line. Unfortunately, that is where the trail ended. The hotel register did not reveal any credible link to a potential suspect. There was no videotape outside the inn to document where he went from there. His tire tracks abruptly ended as well.

Doc said, "It was actually a very odd thing. It was as if the vehicle had simply disappeared."

We all sat in silence. To myself I questioned Doc's comment, " … simply disappeared?"

"Or," I said out loud, "maybe it was transported." With all eyes on me, I expanded my thoughts.

"Maybe it was loaded onto a trailer of some sort and taken away. Were there any other identifiable tracks in the area?" This was sort of a wild, off-the-cuff theory but worth a thought.

Doc Marvin suggested that this was actually a very reasonable scenario. Apparently, however, no other tracks had been collected, which was rather disappointing to learn. But this certainly would explain why the tracks had just disappeared the way they did.

"But what would be the purpose?" asked Chief Jeremy.

"Good question!" I responded. "Maybe his vehicle broke down. Maybe we should be looking for a tow truck. Maybe even a second driver."

I continued, "Another consideration is that we are assuming that the trailer is open and visible to passersby. Maybe it's actually enclosed so you can't see what is inside ... like a semi or other large truck."

As we considered these very viable concepts, there was a strong consensus among the group that the suspect may be hiding the vehicle he used in the commission of his crimes. "That may be part of his M.O. We knew he used the same vehicle since similar track patterns had been found at various locations where he was known to have been. But now we questioned how he got it there and why he went to all the trouble that we believed he had. Maybe he had some kind of emotional attachment to the vehicle. Could this also be part of his signature? It seemed like each new question found us asking ten more. But, out of all the questions, one thing was for sure. The vehicle was significant to the crimes for some reason.

We had to get closer to identifying it," I thought. "But how?"

Before changing topic, it was determined that we would follow up with tow truck services that may have responded to a disabled vehicle call at the Inn in question. We knew this may be a needle in a haystack, but we just may find that we get lucky. And, if not, then we could eliminate that theory altogether and focus on the trailer or truck concept.

Doc Marvin continued with his presentation. Moving onto another thought altogether, he commented that in all three cases, the victims had been swimming in the waters of Lake Erie prior to their deaths. He posed the question we had all been thinking.

"Why would they swim in dirty lake water after swimming in a nice clean pool? I want you all to consider this as you proceed with the investigation."

I **had** thought about this. I had actually given it a lot of thought. Recalling that Anna had been training for a triathlon, it led me to think about open water swimming as part of the overall competition. Recognizing her need to train in this environment, her connection to swimming in the lake was understandable. But the question remained, what about the others? Obviously, this was another follow-up detail we couldn't ignore.

As the meeting progressed, Doc Marvin introduced Tia Thomas, the trace evidence expert with whom he had been working. Tia was known for her keen eye for detail; she was adept at recognizing the significance of the slightest elements. They worked together as well as with a highly trained footwear and tire track examiner. Doc Marvin deferred his comments to Tia for the remainder of the briefing.

Tia pointed out that in each case, numerous sneaker prints were found in the muddy alcove areas where the vehicles were parked. Castings had been taken, but because each of the areas was frequented during the day by the public, our initial assessment was that they would be of little benefit in connecting the prints to a suspect with any credibility. Tia, however, looked closely at the depth of depression and weight distribution in each print. Through her expertise and particular testing techniques, she was able to determine that at least one print from each location was made by a common individual.

Tia pulled up several photos of footprints on the overhead screen. Pointing to the outsoles, they were absent of any specific logo. She was hopeful, however, that the grooves and patterns could be traced back to a single manufacturer due to patent protections on the design. She also pointed out a slight scuff pattern on the bottoms of the shoes. The pattern impressions were indicative of the suspect's style of walking and would be unique to our suspect.

So, what did these footprints tell us? We knew what size shoe the perpetrator wore ... an average men's US size 10. We also knew that he scuffed his feet when he walked and that he walked with a limp on his right leg. Individually, these findings may not seem like much. But cumulatively, this information would prove useful to law enforcement officials when identifying the perp as well as when presenting it as court evidence. While we continued to refine the profile of our suspect, the limp would corroborate my theory that the guy we were looking for had some type of physical limitation.

Doc Marvin and Tia also took a close look at the tire prints found at the scene. They zeroed in on the print evidence taken not only from the same alcove area as the footprints but also the surrounding area. Again, Tia was successful in identifying a common tire print that occurred in all three locations. Furthermore, by reviewing the tread patterns, they were able to narrow down the tire to a specific manufacturer, which helped them to determine the size and type of tire. Tia displayed a photo of an 185/70R14 tire and explained that this type of tire was commonly used on compact cars and sedans. With the tire size identified, they took a closer look at the track, which is the distance between tires. By analyzing the spatial relationship between the tire tracks, they were able to determine the wheelbase and turning diameter of the vehicle. With a wheelbase of 100.1 inches, they now knew that the vehicle was most likely a sedan.

While this didn't seem like it narrowed our search down very much, considering the number of vehicles out on the road, it did. Each new detail we were able to uncover helped us unravel a bit more of the puzzle, leading us closer to identifying our perp.

Tia concluded the briefing by affirming that a full analysis of the tire tread and track was expected to reveal key details of the vehicle we were looking for. That, along with the wear and markings unique to the tires, would ultimately prove to be strong evidence in connecting our perp and his vehicle to the crimes.

Headway was being made, but it had been an exhaustingly late day at the office. Falling into the comfort of my bed was a well-deserved and welcome relief. As I sank into the lush, thick foam mattress, I pulled the feather-filled duvet up over my shoulders. My tired body melted into the covers as thoughts of the day swirled around in my head.

As I slowly drifted off to sleep, my final waking thoughts were spent pondering over all the tiny little fingerprints we leave behind in our everyday lives. Whether it be from picking up a glass, walking into a room, or even by shedding a single, solitary hair, we leave these remnants unknowingly and without cause. It's a powerful reality to understand that these marks tell a story. They tell *your* story, even when you're oblivious that you left them behind. Both intriguing and chilling at the same time, it only takes one person to read that story and unlock the secrets held in your DNA.

In the shallows of my mind, I thought how, in today's world, *this could be a blessing ... or ... it could be a curse.*

CHAPTER 18

Tick Tock

Tuesday, July 30, 2024

Tuesday morning started like any other day. Rising to the chirping of the birds and enjoying a nice warm cup of coffee, the weather forecast called for another warm and sunny day. I expected it to be a busy day and wanted to get an early start. With a quick shower and brush of the teeth, I threw on my cap and shades and was headed out the door.

The Police Department in Ackerton was bustling this particular morning. The local officers were dealing with an early morning drug bust and several DWIs from the night before, while the War Room had taken on a life of its own. The chatter in the halls and sounds emanating from the offices were quite exhilarating, and I knew, at that moment, we would succeed in cracking this case. This was exactly the energy we needed to keep this investigation moving forward.

It wasn't my intention to spend the day analyzing the recording found on Anna's cell phone but, my inquiring mind wanted to know. I could not wait another moment as I settled into my office chair with the phone and tissues in hand. Needless to say, this would prove to be one of the most heart-wrenching experiences I've had to endure over all my years of working with violent crimes. I have dealt with many graphic cases, but this one was tugging on my heartstrings. The contents of the recording confirmed everything I had already believed to be true about our perpetrator and would serve as a huge piece of evidence once caught.

It began with Anna conversing with a male voice. It was nothing forced, just a casual conversation. It was apparent that Anna was there of her own free will. They were discussing the details of a swimmer's training program, referred to only as ASTI. The male voice was promising to increase swim times in both confined and open waters. He talked about an eight-week camp at an east coast college.

He was a convincing salesman, and as the conversation progressed, Anna's voice grew questionably more uncertain. You could hear the hesitation creep into her voice, as, I'm sure, her male encounter could as well. She began to ask generic questions. Mostly, they went

176

unanswered, but even with no response, she was giving us clues about her assailant.

"Eres español," Anna said. To which he responded, "Si." She had asked if he was Spanish, to which he replied, "Yes."

"How long have you been recruiting? Wouldn't you like to retire?"

"What kind of car is that? I love vintage cars! And those windows … they are almost as black as the shiny coat."

As she made an excuse to leave, his disposition shifted significantly. Her attempt was followed by what sounded like a small scuffle, and in a heightened expression, you could hear Anna's voice yell, "Ouch!"

We assumed she had been seated next to him when he jabbed her in the leg with the paralytic agent. Due to its ability to quickly subdue the victim, all he had to do was gently lay her down on the slated rock. The remainder of the tape consisted of his voice talking to her. There was no response from her. In the beginning, his words were gentle, almost compassionate, as he gave her a play-by-play of everything he was doing. But it didn't take long for his character to shift toward a more demeaning, unscrupulous, and increasingly aggressive tone. Of particular interest was the name, Susan. He referred to Anna as Susan several times during the recording. And as his demeanor became more aggressive, he called out that name in a belligerent and hostile manner. The sounds of her assault were gross and vulgar. The recording ceased but not before you heard disgustingly vile groans, the foul sounds of heavy breathing, and a distant echo of crashing waves.

I sat with both elbows propped on the table in front of me. My forehead rested in the palm of my hands. My eyes were closed, imagining the events that had taken place. Both Colin and Chief Jeremy had joined me early on while listening to the recording; neither knew what to say. There really was nothing anyone could say and I appreciated their silence while I processed what we had just heard. This would probably be the only time that we were all at a loss for words.

After wiping the tears from my eyes and once I was able to gather my thoughts, I suggested that we look into the name of the swim camp. Chief Jeremy confirmed that they had already been looking, but so far, none had been identified that matched with the acronym ASTI. They would continue to search for a match but were not confident that one would turn up.

"Likely, a fictitious camp," he stated.

"What about the college?" I asked.

Chief Jeremy confirmed that they had already been in contact with the university. There was no ongoing recruitment activity for any part of their swim program; in fact, there hadn't been in the past few years. They were actually in the final year of phasing out their swim program altogether. They were, however, working on getting us a historical list of all recruiters since the inception of the program. This may be where our perp's behavior had to evolve. Maybe he filled the role of recruiter and had to keep up the façade when the program was eliminated.

Just then, the technical expert who supports our online research entered the room. Excusing herself for the interruption, she felt she had important information for us to consider. While exploring the vastness of the internet, she came across what she believed was a bogus website; one that matched the acronym we were looking for. Interestingly, she confirmed that there had been no success in tracking the website's originating IP address.

She stated, "ASTI. It stands for American Swimmer's Training Institute."

She pointed out a link at the bottom of the page. The link redirected the reader to the college in question. However, once at the college website, there was no way to go back to the ASTI page. The only way to get back to the ASTI page was to type the full website address in a new internet search window. In looking at the coding of the page, she believed it was not a legitimate website. This was extremely important since this would support the theory of a fictitious training camp. The college link offered the reader some legitimacy, without the campus ever realizing the link existed. A creatively smart move that even a novice web designer could accomplish. However, the content creator, though skilled in their attempt to hide the website from common traffic, didn't consider we'd get this far in the investigation. It was, in large part, thanks to Anna. Without her help from beyond the grave, we never would have so many details about her attacker.

Moving forward, I decided to take a deeper look at the topic of open swimming and what the significance might have been to each of our victims.

In my research, I learned that open swimming can enhance a swimmer's training in many ways that swimming in a pool cannot. Open swimming can more easily identify stroke imbalances that require correction. This is particularly important when a swimmer does not have the bottom of the pool to look toward for guidance. There is other evidence that shows open water swimming can boost the immune system, improve mood, and reduce stress. It also shows promising benefits to the heart by increasing circulation and can develop balance and core strength.

Fitness levels will also tend to improve. By performing in harsh conditions, the body will learn to react quicker. The temperature of the water itself helps with this since swimming in colder water makes breathing more difficult. Training in these conditions forces the body to optimize what little oxygen the swimmer is taking in and helps them to adapt to the stressful conditions.

The temperature of the water, waves, currents, tides, wind, sun, and even obstacles all add unique challenges for the swimmer. Even if the swimmer has no desire to compete in open water, the benefit of training offers swimmers the opportunity to improve pool performance. If nothing else, it is believed that the swimmer will develop a mental toughness that will help them push through whatever challenges are thrown at them in the pool.

"This is all very interesting, but how does this tie into our cases?" I thought to myself.

Two things came to mind. First, our perp was obviously well-versed and convincing. If he was able to convince his victims to travel and meet him at a semi-remote location, it would seem he might be quite the salesman. My first thought is that he used his knowledge of the benefits of open swim to sell them on his training program. Maybe he wanted them to experience the transition from a pool to open water in order for them to feel the difference This would, undoubtedly, give his pitch more credibility.

Second, without already having open water training, they would likely become more winded and strain more against the conditions. Maybe he wanted to tire them out, leaving them with little energy and needing to rest on the rock where they had been assaulted.

After this day, physically, I was exhausted. Emotionally, I was drained. It was a welcome relief to arrive at mom's home, with Colin by my side. Dinner was made, pinot noir was poured, and all we had to do was sit back and enjoy the company. The only thing missing was Josie.

"Mom, where's Josie?" I asked.

She said she had an errand to run and would be back in an hour." As Mom looked at the clock over the kitchen sink. "Hmmmmm, that was about two hours ago."

"Mom! Did you tell her to stay away from the campus?" I excitedly asked.

"I didn't think I had to. She was with me all day. Except for doing her errand. She said she was going to stop down at the police station and check in on you when she was done and before coming home." Mom looked concerned.

I was also concerned. "We weren't at the Duncan Station today. I never saw her." I grabbed my phone and proceeded to dial her number.

Ring … ring … ring. No answer. Colin tried to calm my nerves by reassuring me that she was ok; she must have just gotten caught up with her errands. "I'll call the station," he said.

As I paced the floor, my wild imagination had begun taking over. I was clearly losing control of my emotions and letting my thoughts, irrational as they may have been, get the best of me. A frantic feeling came over me at the thought of my daughter becoming the next victim of our already infamous killer.

Tick-tock. Tick-tock. Tick-tock.

Ever so slow, goes the clock.

Especially when you are desperately trying to find someone.

CHAPTER 19

The Secret – Part II

Tuesday, July 30, 2024

Colin re-entered the room with a sigh of relief written all over his face. "She's on her way home," he said with an encouraging smile.

I looked at him, realizing that maybe Anna's case was becoming too much for me. I was reacting in ways that I never had before. I was clearly having a difficult time separating the realities of the crimes in my professional life with the emotional attachments of my personal life. These were a conflict of emotions I had not experienced before. In the past, I had always been capable of separating them.

"Where did you find her?" I asked.

"She was still at the police station," Colin said. "Officer Crane was entertaining her."

"You mean the handsome young officer at the reception desk?" I asked.

"That would be him," Colin replied with a smile.

With a sense of relief, I walked toward him and grabbed his hand. "Again, my savior," I whispered.

Clearly, I was going to have to speak with Josie about open lines of communication, especially in light of the current investigation.

Mom was just as relieved to know that Josie was ok. "I'm sorry, Sonny. I didn't mean to upset you," she said.

"No, Mom. It's me. You did nothing wrong and everything right!"

Mom smiled and suggested we take our conversation and dinner out on the back patio. The stifling air inside was making her claustrophobic and she thought the fresh air would do us good. We were all in agreement.

We had just finished transferring dinner to the back patio when Josie arrived. Lighthearted, lovely Josie. Unaware of the commotion she had just stirred. She gleefully glided in with a cheerful "Hi!" I couldn't help but smile at her unassuming ways. She had always been such a mild-mannered girl, completely oblivious to the dangers of life that lurked outside of her protective walls. Walls that I had built. Which, at this point in life, may or may not be a good thing.

"I met the sweetest officer at the station!" Josie announced, grinning from ear to ear.

"Officer Crane. He is a good man with a promising future in law enforcement," Colin nodded, acknowledging his approval.

Dinner was superb! It was no surprise since this was the usual result of my mother's cooking. I hadn't had her *city chicken* since I was a child. It was one of my favorite dishes. I'm sure that's why she made it. She'd allowed me to reminisce, while sharing one of my beloved dishes with my children.

I could see my kids eyeing the meal on a stick, not quite sure what to make of it. "Just try it!" Mom encouraged them.

So, one by one they took a little nibble to see what this unique dish was all about. I was happy to see it was to their liking. Mom explained that it was like deep-fried chicken on a stick. The stick made it fun to eat. But I knew that, traditionally, it was more than just chicken. It was actually made with cubes of pork on a small skewer, coated in breading, and both fried and baked to a delicate crisp. The original recipe called for pork **and** veal, but I adamantly protested the use of veal as a child, so mom resorted to making the dish solely with pork.

"Was I spoiled much? Not at all!" I chuckled to myself.

Combined with the aroma of hot baked mac and cheese, both satisfied my craving for comfort food. If that wasn't enough, she served a side of fresh cucumber salad and homemade bread.

As we filled our bellies to the brim, we couldn't forget about dessert. Mom would never forget dessert! On the menu was strawberry shortcake with whipped cream topping, made from scratch. Her sponge cakes melted in our mouths, while the sweetness of the fruit topping teased the palate. She always outdid herself. After all these years, I should have come home **just** for her cooking.

"Yum!!" I exclaimed! "Why is it that our mother's cooking is always better than our own?"

I wasn't the only one enjoying the feast. By the looks on everyone's faces, we all shared the same sentiment.

With the satiating meal and enlightening conversation winding down, I noticed the twins eyeing the whipped cream. Watching their expressions, I had a great idea about how we could utilize the leftovers.

"Mom's old board game. I played it as a kid," I thought.

I knew she still had it because I saw it tucked away in the hallway closet. It was the original 1969 version of a popular remake they had for sale in the stores. Recognizing it probably held collector's value, I went to retrieve it anyway. The kids had never played it before and I was sure they would find it as entertaining as I once had.

And I was right! It was the hit of the night! One by one we planted our chins on the designated headrest, prepared to receive a whipped cream pie in our faces. Would we have to crank the handle one time or six? The number of clicks each of us would make would be determined by a roll of that tiny, little dice. Eventually, one of the clicks would release the hand holding the whipped cream pie, and voila! The recipient got blasted with a whipped cream pie in their face! It was a hysterically comical end to an amazing evening. This was much needed after the events of earlier in the day.

After the boys went to bed, Josie and Mom withdrew to the living room. Both had a mad passion for nostalgic movies. I'm sure my mother was in her glory, being able to share her favorite pastime with someone else. That gave Colin and me a bit of alone time as we retreated to the large pavilion located at the far back corner of the yard. It was the perfect place for us to steal a private moment. The same partially enclosed space we would run off to so many times before, in our early years of dating. It sported a steep domed roof and screened walls that would allow for a 360-degree view of the outside. Constructed of natural wood, this Amish-made structure was the perfect spot when in search of some peaceful seclusion.

We quickly settled into the comfortable outdoor sofa, giggling like the school kids we once were. How comforting it was to be back here after all those years. With no electrical power, it was only illuminated by the light of the moon. Colin assertively and passionately kissed me ... my neck, my face, my lips. It did not take us long before we were treading familiar territory, stumbling in the dark, as we groped for each other's bodies.

"A quickie will have to do." I whispered as I lifted my skirt.

We eagerly entwined and instantly became one rhythmic movement.

Completely out of breath, Colin lay silently atop of me. I wished I could have savored that moment forever. Straight out of the movies, we had snuck off to steal a kiss ... like two carefree teens running wildly in the night. Surrounded by the expanse of the fresh, open air and the soft, soothing sounds of nature, we got ensnared in a physical attraction far too strong to deny. Risking that we might get caught at any time, the adrenaline pumped through our veins sharing in the climactic moment when our two bodies had become one.

In the comfort of each other's arms, it was a beautiful and peaceful moment. Few places exist where you can lay back and listen to a chorus of crickets as you are surrounded in song. It was incredible.

Suddenly, out of nowhere, Colin broke the silence.

"How old is Josie?" he asked.

Taken aback by the question, I thought it was a bit out of place for the moment. But I responded anyway, "She's nineteen years old, why?"

"Nineteen?" he asked.

"Yes, why?" I repeated.

"Because I have been thinking. I haven't been able to get this out of my mind," Colin said.

I tried to see his expression, but it was difficult in the dark. It was evident, though, that there was a serious, yet worrying quiver in his voice. He continued, "Do you know who her father is?"

I paused in silence as a knot developed in the depths of my stomach. Had I had something in my mouth, I'm sure

I would have spit it out. "The rest of my secret," I thought.

I hadn't expected to discuss this after such a wonderful evening, and certainly not immediately following an intimate moment. But the time was here, and the time was now.

I cleared my throat. "Well, remember my secret? The reason why I left Duncan?"

"Yes," he replied.

"I believe that Josie's father is the man who raped me."

Colin gasped. "Sonny! Oh Sonny!"

Before he could continue, I immediately interrupted. "I have always been honest with her ... well, as honest as I could be. I explained away her conception as one that resulted from an ill-fated union. Due to inexplicable circumstances, I was clear that he would not be a part of her life. I always reinforced that no matter what the circumstances were surrounding her conception, she was no accident. God had been watching out for both of us. He made sure she had a father who would love her and raise her. That was the father she found in Devon."

I continued, "Dear, sweet Josie. She never questioned it. She accepted this scenario and sought joy and appreciation in what she had versus what she didn't have."

Colin remained compassionate and understanding. He admired how I had handled the situation with Josie. But still, he seemed a bit troubled by my response, and he didn't waste any time making his apprehension known. Ultimately, he suggested that **he**, in fact, could be her father.

I really had never considered him as an option. I think I had been so caught up in the trauma I was dealing with that I had only considered that she was the result of the rape. I reminded him how careful we had always been. Considering our meticulous planning, I didn't feel there was any way he could have fathered her. Surely, if I thought he had, I would have reached out to him.

Colin thoroughly understood and respected my thinking but insisted that he wanted to perform a DNA test. This must have been weighing on his mind since my first mention of my daughter.

"We were like rabbits, Sonny. Don't you remember? It is possible that something slipped by and I could be the father." He adamantly reminded me. "Don't you want to know? I want to know."

I was so torn as to what to do. On one hand, I was excited at the thought of him being her father. But, in my mind, that was just a fantasy. In reality, I knew that was not the likely scenario. I was extremely fearful of getting my hopes up, only to have them come crashing down. I had spent all these years convinced that Josie was born from the seed of my attacker; how do you do a 180-degree turn away from that mindset?

Knowing how confusing this was for me, I couldn't even begin to imagine how emotional this would be for Josie. I have spent a lifetime believing that she was the product of a horrific act. I have also spent a lifetime reframing that scenario into something that I was able to convince both her and myself had been a blessing in disguise.`

I didn't say no; I didn't say yes. I knew this was important to Colin. I knew this could also be a turning point for us, depending on how we handled it. On the other hand, I knew its potential impact on my own mental health and well-being, not to mention that of Josie.

This was definitely a twist to the evening that I had not expected. "Let me think about where we go with this, Colin," I said. "Just give me a little time to come to terms with this, ok?"

Colin agreed. He recognized that he had spent all these years never even knowing that Josie existed. He knew he could wait a little longer if he needed to. Somehow, some way, we would figure it out. We would work together in the best interest of everyone, to determine the best possible way to move forward.

CHAPTER 20

Voice of An Angel

Wednesday, July 31, 2024

Rubbing my bleary eyes, I had gotten up before dawn, hoping to arrive at the Ackerton PD early—earlier than my counterparts, at least. I really wanted to devote this day to getting to know the Pennsylvania victim better and reacquainting myself with the Ohio victim. I hated referring to them so impersonally. They both had names. They had families, relationships, hopes, and dreams. They had futures. I wanted to see **them**. Learn who **they** were. I wanted to honor their memory by recognizing that both were far more than *just* victims.

After a quick shower, I threw my hair in a pony and filled my thermos to the brim. The nutty aroma of the freshly brewed coffee was invigorating.

"I sure do drink a lot of coffee," I thought to myself. "I guess there are far worse things I could be drinking, though," so said the creature of habit.

I grabbed my tote bag and scampered out the door. "Wide-eyed and bushy-tailed," I whimsically thought to myself.

I hit the palm of my hand on my forehead and rolled my eyes back, as a slight chuckle escaped my breath.

"I'm sounding just like my mother. Wide-eyed and bushy-tailed? That was so her!"

It's funny how the course of your entire day can be dictated by how it begins. Mine was off to a good start, so I was hopeful that this would be one of those days that followed course.

The drive was a relaxed and pleasant one, with little traffic to speak of. A pearly glow that lit the sky around me, would gently fade as the sun rose in my rearview mirror. Headed west toward Ackerton, I knew it was bound to be another warm and sunny one on this final day in July.

How grateful I was for my mother. She had a whole laundry list of things planned to occupy my kids when I couldn't be there. Personally speaking, my main hope for the day was to get back to Mom's house at a decent hour. The plan was to take Colin's boat out on the water and do a little tubing before the sun went down. The kids and I were looking forward to a little bit of adventure and a whole lot of fun. I was all about making new memories.

So much for my early morning plans of arriving at the office before my counterparts. Apparently, I was not the only one thinking that way. Following right behind me, into my office, was Chief Jeremy. He had a file in his hand as he headed for the conference table. "Got a minute?" he asked.

"Well, good morning to you too," I replied.

We both chuckled. I sauntered over to the table with my coffee in hand. Chief Jeremy laid the file onto the table; it contained forensic results from the secondary, independent laboratory we had hired.

"They've pretty much corroborated everything we already knew," he said.

This would prove to be a good thing should we eventually go to court. With all things remaining consistent, we could build a stronger case. He left me with the file for my perusal. I was interested in its contents but set it on top of my *to-do* pile for now. I was more interested in spending my day getting to know the victims.

Molly was her name. She was the young lady from Pennsylvania. At 22 years young, Fall would have welcomed her into her final year of school towards earning her four-year degree in music. A competitive swimmer her entire life, she managed to accumulate a healthy number of athletic awards and accolades. She was attending college on a full athletic scholarship and was expected to compete in an international swim competition during this next school year. As athletically inclined as she was, though, her true passion was her singing. Gifted in many ways, Molly grew up number four in the pecking order of five children. Raised in a moderately strict, two-parent household, she was known as the free-spirited, adventuresome one. All who met her were greeted by a perpetual smile. Molly had no known enemies and no boyfriends to speak of. She did, however, have quite a following on social media.

The technology expert had gotten me access to her social media accounts. I had spent a couple of hours scrolling through them when I came across one particular video that caught my eye. A beautiful headshot of Molly with a bright and toothy grin was staring back at me from the screen. I took the mouse in my right hand and scrolled it over the play button. Click. The video began to roll.

"Hi! I'm Molly!"

She cheerily greeted her listeners with a warm and inviting smile.

She was sitting on what I assumed to be her bed, hair pulled up in a ponytail, and casually sporting a V-neck tee. I could see a bedroom dresser in the background and walls plastered with a variety of posters.

"Typical room for a girl of her age. Probably her dorm room," I thought.

Her video continued, "I would like to dedicate this song to my father, who has worked so hard for so many years taking care of our family. He was recently involved in a very bad accident and lost both of his legs. He is having a really hard time coming to terms with it and with being unable to support us like he was used to doing. I wrote this for him to remind him of how strong he is and that he can overcome anything. I want him to know … he's my hero!"

With a guitar tucked under her arm, she began to strum. And, as soon as she opened her mouth, I knew exactly why she had such a strong media presence. It was like nothing I had ever heard before. Her voice possessed an airy, yet rich, tonal quality that floated effortlessly through the air. Every ethereal note within her broad vocal range was hit with precision and clarity. Both confident and expressive in her delivery, she offered her heart on a platter. She was a powerful artist that captivated and mesmerized her listeners through the resonant sound of her music. For me, personally, those three short minutes of song managed to transform me into her world and evoked emotions I didn't think were possible.

As the interlude ended, I couldn't help but speak out loud. "Wow! Just incredible!" I was completely enamored by her voice. She had the voice of an angel.

I continued to sit, silently in awe, pondering the melody that echoed from beyond. I felt like everything I ever needed to know about Molly, I'd learned from that one song. She was an old soul, filled with depth and wisdom that was uncommon of a girl her age. To think that this incredibly beautiful and talented young woman had her life cut short by such a demented, narcissistic creep both sickened and angered me.

I got up from my chair and paced around the room. I needed a mental health break before focusing on our other victim.

Patricia, or Tish, as she had been more commonly known, was the very first victim from this case … at least, the first one that we knew of. At the time, of course, we had no idea that she would become part of a serial investigation. We thought hers was an isolated murder in northeastern Ohio; my unit had only become involved upon special request following heavy pressure from multiple news outlets. Unfortunately, we couldn't be of much assistance. With no prints, no DNA, and a squeaky-clean crime scene, there was nothing we could add to their investigation. Tish's murder had gone unsolved for the past three years with no leads … until now. As strange as the red ribbon seemed, our perp's little signature is what caught the attention of the authorities. That's exactly what he wanted, however. In his irrational and crazy mind, he wanted credit for his conquests.

She was twenty-one years old at the time of her death. Her features were similar to both Molly and Anna—dark hair, pale skin, and a petite frame. She grew up the only child of a prominent businessman. Her small farming community kept her humble. A natural-born swimmer, she led her high school team all the way to the nationals. She continued her love of the water throughout college and was hoping to qualify at the Olympic trials in 2022. Along with being on the swim team at her university, she belonged to several campus clubs. Tish ranked top in her class and spent her summers volunteering for a variety of not-for-profit organizations. She had a particular love for animals and aspired to become a veterinary doctor someday. Her ultimate dream, though, was to open an animal rescue on her grandparent's farm.

"What a well-rounded, kind-hearted young woman," I thought to myself. "Equally as beautiful as both Molly and Anna."

I hadn't really expected Tish to have any social media accounts still lingering about. Since her passing was several years ago, the likelihood was a hit or a miss. My recollection from reviewing her case back then was that there wasn't much to be seen. To my surprise, however, the technology expert had located a couple of sources of information still floating out in cyberspace.

I hadn't scrolled long before I came across one very familiar, yet highly unlikely, face among her friends. Both shocked and dismayed, I sat up in my chair. I was intent upon learning what type of connection they had to one another. After researching hundreds upon hundreds of photos, there was nothing—not one picture of them together. This would lead me to believe that they (1) had an old connection, or (2) were mere acquaintances, or (3) didn't really know each other at all. Just then, Colin walked into my somewhat barren, make-shift office.

"Well hello there, Beautiful," he said in a quiet voice, just slightly above a whisper.

He didn't want the others in the station to hear his term of endearment, since we were still running around in hiding. The sound of his voice completely distracted my attention away from the computer screen. Sitting down next to me at the conference table, I greeted him in return.

"Hey Colin," I smiled, and as I did, I leaned in and grabbed a quick snuggle with my cheek against his massive chest.

Returning to my upright position, I could feel the warmth of his hand gently slide between my thighs. Moving his hand back and forth, tenderly caressing, his touch was sensual, yet firm.

"How are you doing in here? Find anything interesting?" he asked as he gave me a little squeeze.

I snuggled against him again. "Mmmmmm, I found **you**," I said in a sultry tone. "**You** interest me," I continued the flirtatious response.

I let out a slight moan as he moved his hand higher up my thigh and squeezed slow and tight. My lower extremities began to tingle as tiny, little butterflies flittered around in my gut.

"Those darn butterflies," I thought to myself.

I reluctantly wreathed myself away. Letting out another quiet moan, I wished we had been somewhere else in that moment ... somewhere other than the Ackerton PD.

"Actually," I said. "Not to change the subject, but I **did** come across something quite interesting." I turned the screen of my computer in his direction. "Who do you see?" I asked.

Colin pulled his hand from my leg and reached for the screen. Looking a bit bewildered, he scanned the photos and zeroed in on one in particular.

He asked, "What is this? What are you showing me?" Furrowing his eyebrows, he wasn't quite sure what to make of it.

I told him that I was on one of Tish's old social media accounts. While scouring through her friend list, I came across this photo.

"You're looking at Tish's friend list! How is this possible?" I asked, still a little flabbergasted.

We looked at each other. Colin's jaw dropped. We were both at a loss for words.

CHAPTER 21

A Familiar Face

Wednesday, August 7, 2024

No matter what the reasoning was, it had been oddly intriguing for Fred's face to have been staring back at us from among Tish's friends.

"Either something really sick and sinister is going on, or, by sheer coincidence, Fred has some really bad luck," I said to Colin.

We both agreed that we would need to talk to Fred. We also agreed that we would keep this between ourselves until we had some answers. We were hugely concerned that the media would have a heyday with this information.

We decided that Colin would do some digging to see if he could ascertain why Fred was listed as one of Tish's social media friends. It certainly was an odd pairing, but maybe there was a reasonable explanation. I couldn't help but wonder, though, what the chances were that Fred would know two of our victims, from two different states, in a case that he had already been named as a suspect. I tried to remind myself that he had a rock-solid alibi for Anna's death. But maybe Fred's alibi was *too* solid. Maybe in the end, it would break apart into a million tiny pieces.

This was not how I wanted the investigation to play out. But sometimes, things need to fall apart before they come back together. I knew that, in this case, I needed to let the pieces fall where they may and be prepared for any possible outcome.

"Let the pieces fall where they may."

I continued to tell myself that over the next week. Unfortunately, Colin was no closer to finding a connection between Tish and Fred than I was to allowing the media to get ahold of this juicy detail. We needed to work harder and smarter. We needed to know why Fred was on Tish's page. I figured it was probably time that I paid Fred a visit myself.

I called Fred and made arrangements to meet him for lunch. I explained to him that there was an update on the case and I needed some insight. I asked if we could meet discreetly so as not to bring unwanted attention to ourselves. Fred suggested we meet at a quaint little place in the heart of Amish country, located about twenty-five miles south of Duncan. It sounded like a good spot.

Within the hour, I was seated at a little table across from Fred. I felt uncomfortable sitting in his presence, but I wasn't sure if it was because of the circumstances under which we were meeting or the fact that I was meeting Emily's husband behind her back. In either case, I would be happy once this encounter was over.

An ivory lace linen delicately covered our table. Its scalloped edging dangled daintily, nearly reaching down to the floor. It was carefully set for two, plated in fine bone china, and accompanied by pristine silver. Delicate floral topiaries featuring freshly cut lavender stood in the center of each table; their fragrance filled the air with aromatic waves of their flowery bloom. There was no doubt that these centerpieces were crafted on-site. Hand-picked from the sprawling lavender fields and wildflower gardens that surrounded us outside, everything about the place hinted of old English charm. From the cottage's stoney façade to the little white picket fence, even the rolling pastures aired on the side of authentic old-world allure. The occasional horse and buggy clickety-clacking by added an additional depth of appeal to this already captivating little place.

Fred and I found ourselves tucked away quietly in a private little corner. I thought to myself that this would be such a wonderful little spot where Colin and I could sneak away. With its warm and romantic appeal, it truly was a hidden gem.

"Do you know why I suggested this place?" Fred asked.

"No. But my guess is you're going to tell me," I replied.

"Because this is where Anna and I would come to eat," he said. "It was our secret little spot where we could sit freely and just be ourselves."

I wasn't going to allow myself to sympathize with Fred. I still did not like him very much. He was a shallow man. Nevertheless, I needed to be nice to him because, ultimately, I needed something from him. I pulled a piece of paper from my purse and held it in front of his face. It was a screenshot of Tish's friend list with his profile picture among a number of others. "Do you want to explain this? " I asked.

Fred observed the photo and took the paper from my hand. He adjusted his glasses and pulled it closer. "It's a picture of me. Where did you get this?" Fred inquired.

He looked genuinely baffled. I explained where the screenshot had originated from, and he chuckled. "Why are you laughing, Fred? This is serious!" I demanded.

"I'm not sure what is so serious about this. Patricia is a cousin of a cousin of a cousin ... or something like that," Fred explained. "She found me on one of those DNA sites. Apparently, we were a match at some level. We shared a few messages about our family trees, and then she requested my friendship on this site. So, I added her."

I looked at him in disbelief.

"And that's it!" he exclaimed.

"That's it?" I asked.

"That's the last time I ever heard from her," he continued. "That was years ago. I never even met the girl. I'm never on that site and honestly forgot I even had an account on there."

"How many years ago, Fred?" I continued.

"I don't know! Maybe four or five. What is this all about?" he asked.

"Just an FYI ... Patricia goes by the name of Tish," I said in a defensive tone. "Did you know that Tish passed away three years ago?"

Fred adamantly rejected the idea that he had any knowledge of her passing. He was shocked to learn that she was a victim of murder and even more shocked to find out that she was murdered by the same man who killed Anna. He was so believable. Nothing in his body language or facial expressions said he was being dishonest. Still, I took his word with a grain of salt; I reminded myself that narcissists are believable too.

We had just finished our lunch when I placed my hands on the table. I was completely taken by surprise when Fred reached across the table and took my hands in his. I furrowed my brow and looked at him, wondering what he was doing. As I pulled slowly back, releasing his hold, he leaned further forward and grabbed my hands again, cupping mine in his.

He gazed into my eyes, or at least he *tried* to, and said, "You know I've always admired you, Sonny. I even had a thing for you at one point. If there is anything you need … anything at all, I'm here for you."

I wanted to gag as I broke his gaze and jerked my hands back. This time I pulled them completely off the table. "Was he making a pass at me?" I thought. "Now I was **really** feeling uncomfortable."

I didn't even respond to his comment and quickly excused myself from the table. I thanked him for meeting with me, left money for the bill, and hurried out the door.

Back in my car, I immediately called Colin. I was clearly rattled as I explained to him what had just happened. I told him that while Fred would likely dismiss his actions as a gesture of friendship, he and I both knew exactly what he meant.

"Ew!" I burst out loud.

Colin chuckled.

I was slightly offended by the chuckle, but then I understood that what Colin found comical was my reaction, not Fred's advance. He was clearly disturbed by Fred's forwardness and instructed me to never be alone in his presence again. And then, in a turn of events, Colin had become genuinely upset with me.

"What if Fred was the killer? Why would you meet him in a secluded location? All alone! Why would you go there and not tell me or anyone where you were going?"

He fumed in an aggressive voice.

Yeah, he was clearly angry. But I deserved it. He was absolutely right. I had been careless, and I understood that his anger was coming from a place deep within his heart. I remained submissive to his rant, and once he said what he needed to say, it was done. His show of masculinity only served to strengthen the yearning attraction I already felt.

In another turn of events, this past week brought a bit more transparency about our mystery man from the swimming pool. Investigators had obtained numerous video clips from public sources as they tried to piece together the routes that the victims and suspect had taken. Zooming in on the clips obtained, our analysts were able to get a relatively clear side view of the vehicle he was driving. They identified it as a four-door, vintage K-car. It was black in color with deeply tinted windows. A look back at the analysis of the tire tracks and tread proved consistent with this finding. Now we had a vehicle. So where was it?

Recognizing that there may not be many on the road, our analysts did a thorough search of the motor vehicle registration records across the country. They felt it surely must have been registered somewhere. Our guys got a few hits but nothing that really amounted to anything. All the vehicles were geographically located too far outside our radius of interest. This would reinforce our belief that the perp was only bringing it out on public roads when committing his crimes. It was likely being stored somewhere centrally located to the murders. That would place it somewhere in Pennsylvania. But, a review of the highway webcam footage shot around the time of Anna's and Molly's murders, turned up nothing. So, we knew he wasn't driving it on public highways. This brought us back to our theory that the suspect may be transporting it for use in the murders.

With regard to the lack of registration, the theory emerged that he may have rebuilt it from a salvaged title, allowing him to stay under the radar. Considering this scenario, he likely failed to register it once it became roadworthy. On the bright side, though, at least this new knowledge brought us a little closer to finding him. Captain Jeremy sent out an APB for law enforcement to be on the lookout for this unique vintage car. It wouldn't be hard to miss once spotted.

Thinking about the vehicle, my thoughts roamed back to Fred. "What if **he** had a vintage K-car?" I thought. I reminded myself not to get too carried away in my thinking, but I couldn't help but wonder what was in that huge barn that sat in the back of their property. "It certainly was big enough to house a large truck," I thought.

"Enough, Sony! Enough of this craziness!" I needed to refocus my thinking and not let my mind wander.

So, I switched my train of thought to home. So much was going on. I only had a few more days with the boys before they went back to stay with their father in Virginia. School would be starting, and they were excited about entering the fourth grade. Josie would be off to school herself with the promise of returning for the holidays. Needless to say, my mother was ecstatic to have her return over winter break. Part of me, however, wondered if her return didn't, in part, have something to do with the handsome officer at the Duncan PD.

It had been a week since Colin questioned Josie's paternity. Between the progress we were making on the case and the time being spent with my children, I had little time to think about much else. Colin had been patient, though. He hadn't brought it up again, and I knew it weighed heavily on his heart and his mind.

Back at home and sitting peacefully on Mom's front porch, I could hear the pitter-patter of rain droplets falling rhythmically on the roof. The wind picked up and sent a whistling breeze through the windows. The trees rustled outside while flashes of lightning lit up the room. And then came the roll of thunder, stretching its rumble across the darkening sky. As dreary as the weather seemed to be this evening, it actually offered a welcoming calm.

As I sat in silence, pondering another glass of wine, it struck me! "I had the answer! I knew how we could handle the situation with Josie's paternity! I had the solution!"

I reached for my phone. I was excited to share my epiphany with Colin.

It was awfully late. But I dialed his number anyway.

"Answer your phone, Colin! Just answer your phone." Tap, tap, tapping my fingernail on the bedstand. "Would you please answer your phone?"

"You have reached Officer Griffin. If you have received this message, I am either away from my desk or

213

on another call. Please leave a detailed message, and I will get back to you as soon as I can. Thank you." Beep!

I hung up the phone.

Again, I dialed Colin's number. Ring-ring! Ring-ring! Pause. Ring-ring! Ring-ring! Pause. Still, no answer. My excitement would have to wait, as I snuggled beneath the sheets of my comfy twin-sized bed.

CHAPTER 22

Free Falling

Thursday, August 8, 2024

I had no more than closed my eyes when the first rays of the day peeked into my room. Bathed in soft golden hues, these first streaks of light kissed our sleepy little town and would soon bring it to life. The morning would unfold like the petals of a flower emerging at dawn. Peaceful and rested, I awakened with a fresh sense of purpose.

My phone rang.

As I fumbled for my cell phone, I could see on the ID that it was Colin. I greeted him as I heard his voice on the other end of the line. "What's going on, Sonny? Is everything ok?"

"Everything is fine, Colin! I've had an epiphany!"

"A what?" he asked.

"An epiphany," I laughed.

I went on to explain that this *aha* moment of mine would get him the answer he wanted on Josie's paternity. "It was actually all thanks to Fred," I said.

I explained that I had been thinking about something Fred had said when I met with him for lunch. He had described his connection with Tish as one that was born out of submitting his DNA to one of those sites that allow you to trace your family history. That triggered my own recollection that when Josie was just a little girl, I had submitted her saliva sample to a similar site under an account in my name. I used a fictitious name for her in the hopes that one day I might find a connection that would lead me to the man who raped me. She never knew I had done that. And after several years with no major matches, I completely lost sight of the fact that I had even done it.

My thought was that Colin could submit his DNA sample to the same site. Josie would never have to know, and he could get his answer about paternity. If there was a match between them, it would show up as a relationship. More than likely, however, he'd come to find there wasn't one, and he could forget this crazy notion. I, obviously, had little confidence that Colin was her father. Back in the day, I considered my limited options, and he really wasn't one of them. Based on my calculation of conception, the more likely result was that of my attacker. Combined with the careful protections Colin and I had taken, my view of paternity was solidified. At the very least, however, Colin's thoughts and concerns would be alleviated.

Colin was very agreeable to handling this situation in the manner I was suggesting. How could he not be? It really was an ingenious way to satisfy both our concerns. He immediately went online and ordered his DNA testing kit. It would arrive within seven days. Now, the anticipation that would span weeks of waiting could begin.

Meanwhile, back in the War Room, we weren't sure if we were taking two steps forward and three back or three steps forward and two back. Forensics had confirmed the use of vecuronium with Molly, the Pennsylvania victim. They had also been researching the additional cases I previously identified and determined that they were, in fact, related to the three we were already looking at. I corroborated their findings, and we now had five victims across three states, without any credible suspects. The DNA samples from the epithelial cells retrieved from Anna would return no match. The photo identification software also returned no match. This would indicate that we were dealing with someone who possessed no prior arrest record and who easily integrated with society ... just one more thing to make the process of unmasking our murderer more difficult.

Just as it seemed we were hitting a brick wall, one of our analysts would aid us in taking three giant leaps forward. She had noted the same person appearing in multiple crime scene photos. Bingo! I was correct when I noted that our perp likely revisited the crime scene. She brought me the photos, and as I looked them over, there among the bystanders in the background at several of the scenes was our mystery man. This was the same man that appeared in Anna's photos and likely the same man that Witness Valerie had spotted. Remarkably, this was also the same man who approached me at Anna's funeral luncheon. While it didn't surprise me that he would show up in some of the backgrounds, the audacity it took to approach me directly was unnerving. Had he known who I was all along?

Interestingly, each time he allowed himself to be seen, he was wearing the same set of dark sunglasses. That is, with the exception of when he approached me at Anna's after-funeral luncheon. Witness Valerie and I had both gotten a glimpse of what lay behind those shades. We had seen the same unsettling look. They say that the eyes are the windows to our souls. I'm guessing that our perp knew exactly that, which is why he kept his hidden.

I was feeling positive since we now had a face for our prime suspect. The name and his location would soon follow. Although we had a face to work with, we decided not to release it to the public. We knew that whatever information we released to them, we also released to him. We didn't want to spook him and send him into

218

hiding. All we could do was wait and hope that another clue would reveal itself … and reveal itself soon.

We had made some progress, though. Earlier in the week, one of the team analysts had done a query on the dates of each crime. They had determined that each death had coincided with a full moon. To date, we had amassed a list of five young women who were killed or went missing on or about a full moon. This seemed more planned than coincidental, and we knew that another would be upon us in less than two weeks. We were on high alert in all U.S. states that bordered along the Lake Erie coastline and on particularly high alert in those areas that were located within close proximity to a university facility. Our current list, including estimated date of death, consisted of:

Anna Lee Leone – Duncan, NY – 6/21/24

Molly Johansen – Ackerton, PA – 5/23/24

Patricia "Tish" Emerling – Clinton, OH – 6/24/21

Toni Schnelling (OH Victim 2), Ula, OH – 7/10/17

Lucille Jones (PA Victim 2), Topeka, PA – 8/10/14

We expected this list to grow. Based on the information and evidence we had accumulated, our search had widened. We had expanded it to include all missing persons and unsolved murders that had occurred during the months of April through October, along the U.S. Lake Erie border, over the past twenty years. With that information, we could narrow it down and categorize those cases that occurred on or around a full moon as high-priority reviews. After tonight, we only have three more full moons left in the year that could potentially be used as murder dates. This was due to the fact that the weather would soon become too cold for victims to be *willing* to swim in Lake Erie, which seemed to be a precursor to all of their deaths.

I had to ask myself though, "Why the full moon?"

The most logical conclusion I could surmise was the fact that during the different phases of the moon, its gravitational pull changes. As it comes closer to the Earth, larger bodies of water respond to that change with higher tides. Our suspect wanted his victims to swim in the lake. But why? Could the tides have something to do with it? I could think with all the logic in the world, but realistically, there was nothing logical about these crimes ... except to the *one* with the illogical mind ... the one who was committing them.

With the end of the kids' visit around the corner, Colin and I decided to leave work a little early and spend the rest of the day with them. The afternoon would see us out on the open waters of Lake Erie. Like skidding across a plane of glass, we traveled out to a remote little island unknown to most boaters. But Colin knew; he knew all the best places. He anchored us as close to shore as he could get, after which we all exited the boat and headed out in search of the beach.

The sand was pristine and warm between my toes. The beach itself was small, but it was surrounded by lush green foliage. A plethora of plants and trees provided the backdrop for this delightful little shoreline. The view was incredible with the light puffy clouds floating above the clear blue waters.

"Do you know why I brought you here?" Colin asked.

With a look around, it seemed obvious why he brought us there. He looked at me and said, "Look down."

As I did so, I realized that I was standing on an unscathed beach, abounding with the most beautiful array of beach glass I had ever seen. He remembered that was one of my favorite pastimes. He remembered how, in our younger days, I would get lost for hours on the beaches of Lake Erie. With the schedule I had been keeping, there had been very little 'me' time. I was genuinely touched, and once I had laid my eyes on the ground, I couldn't take them away.

I could have spent a week there, just searching for beach glass, fossils, and little treasures. Any time I walked the beach, my mind would go blank, and any troubles I had would temporarily slip away. The kids enjoyed beach glassing too. I introduced all of them to this hobby on various vacations we had taken. But the highlight of our little adventure wouldn't be the tiny little treasures I dug out of the sand. Instead, it would be the net and volleyball that Colin brought along on the boat.

I don't remember the last time I had laughed so hard. Somehow, it turned into a guys versus gals thing. While I'd love to say we squashed them, we were at their mercy pretty much the entire time. Josie and I gave it our best, but we were no match for Jayce, Jackson, and Colin. They humorously implored that we bow down to them ... submit to their superiority. As much as we struggled, we weren't giving up that easily. We fought the good fight ... right up until the end.

After a fun-filled day, we enjoyed yet another beautiful Lake Erie sunset on our way back home. Lounging back in the boat, arms stretched out beside me, the breeze blew my hair as the water sprayed a light mist upon my face. Tilting my head back, I closed my eyes with my face to the setting sun. I couldn't help but lament on our day. I thought about all that I had missed over the years but loved what life was bringing to me now. Taking in a deep breath of the crisp, clean air, I exhaled in a true sense of relaxation. Lost in my thoughts, I reflected, "I guess it is true ... some things need to fall apart before they fall together."

I was free-falling ... and I loved every minute of it.

CHAPTER 23

Three More Moons

Sunday, August 11, 2024

The dreaded day had finally arrived. I would be putting my beloved Jayce and Jackson on a plane headed back to Virginia. There they would join their dad and his family until this case was solved and I was able to return. They complained the entire morning. They didn't want to leave. Back in Virginia, they had greater restrictions on where and when they could play. In Duncan, they enjoyed the freedom of playing in the neighborhood backyards and had managed to forge a few new friendships during their short stay. I hated to see them go and promised that they could come back for every vacation if they wanted to. It didn't quite make up for having to leave, but it did give them some comfort in knowing they'd be back.

Mom was a wreck. Good-byes were always her biggest weakness.

It was a somber hour-long drive to the airport. I was relieved they had a morning flight since the weather forecast predicted a turn for the worse later that afternoon. We were quickly approaching hurricane season in some of the southern states; this time of year usually brought bad weather along the rest of the east coast as well. Their flight would basically amount to a hop, skip, and a jump, so they were expected to arrive at Devon's well before the bad weather would arrive.

Colin knew I was sad to see them go. After their safe departure, the ride back began as a somber one. But Colin was never one to stay silent. He wasn't one to let a gray cloud hover over anyone's head. In his upbeat and optimistic way, he began revisiting the funny moments we had while the boys had been here. I couldn't believe he had me actually laughing. He recalled how a seagull had pooped on Jackson's head while we were out boating. In the vastness of the Great Lake, the lone seagull found one tiny place to dump, and it just so happened to be right on his head. Although Jackson didn't welcome it at the time, once we cleaned the white slime out of his hair, he grew to appreciate the humor in it.

I said to Colin, "Or, how about when you split your pants going into the restaurant?"

We laughed hysterically together. It was the waitress who would bring it to his attention. What made matters worse was that he decided to go commando that evening. The three-inch split in his seam at the seat of his pants had prominently exposed his bare buns as he strolled through the very crowded eatery. We laughed some more.

"So, what do you think, Sonny? Where do we go from here?" Colin asked.

"What do you mean?" I inquired.

"With us. How do we navigate this? You know we are probably not far from solving this case. How do we keep what we have alive?"

I could tell he was concerned with how the progression of this case would impact our relationship. I was concerned too. My life was back in Virginia … with my kids. My job was back in Virginia too. How does one survive a long-distance relationship? Especially one that is expected to span at least ten years. That is how long it would be before the boys graduated from high school. Would that be fair to Colin? To me? To both of us?

I wasn't really sure how to answer him. "I guess we just have to take it one day at a time," I said. "It's taken a long time, but we've found each other again. That means something, don't you think?"

"I absolutely, 100% agree that it means something, Sonny. I'm willing to work on a long-term relationship with you if you are willing to work on one with me."

This was music to my ears. Of course, I was willing to devote myself to building a long-term future with him. I knew it wouldn't always be easy. But one day at a time, we could work through it. As long as we were on the same page. We would have to plan weekend jaunts to visit with one another. We could take turns, and mine could be on the weekends that I didn't have the boys. It might be expensive, but we both had lucrative incomes, and it certainly was feasible. "The things we do for love." I thought to myself.

I reached over the center console and, with my palm facing upward, opened my hand. Colin responded by placing his own hand on top of mine and clasping it tightly.

"I love you, Sonny."

"I love you too, Colin."

We looked at each other and smiled. This was the first time we both had outwardly expressed our love for one another.

As Colin continued to drive, he took a detour and headed north toward the lake. He drove down a little road, wide enough for only one vehicle. Up ahead was a very old stone archway. The archway was actually a support structure for an antiquated railroad system. As we passed through the structure, paradise came into view … another hidden gem on the Western New York shore of Lake Erie.

Before me stood a sprawling stone structure. If I hadn't known better, I would have guessed it was some type of castle or chateau. There it stood, grandiose in size, with massive pillars greeting you at its front entrance.

"What is this place, Colin?" I asked.

He chuckled. "Well?" he said questioningly. "This is a place I probably should have told you about sooner."

I was completely dumbstruck, having no idea what he was talking about. He would ultimately explain that this place was a dream of his great-great-great-grandfather, who began constructing it when he arrived in the United States in the mid-1800s. He immigrated from Ireland as a wealthy businessman who came to own many plots of land and properties. He had acquired this property in a gambling bet and proceeded to build a dream home for the love of his life. Unfortunately, as soon as he completed the exterior of his fortress, she would succumb to cholera. She left him brokenhearted and the sole caretaker of their three young children.

227

Colin explained, "Although he married for convenience after that, he never fully recovered from the loss of his first wife, my great-great-great-grandmother. He left the interior unfinished, too heartbroken to return to its walls. It has sat in my family for many years, with each generation having a hand in finishing it to what it is today. Ultimately, it has ended up with me."

"Why didn't you tell me about it?" I asked.

Colin continued to share that he didn't come out to *the beach casa* very often and he had never stayed in it before. In fact, it had never actually been lived in.

He said he never really gave it a whole lot of thought, but he added, "Due to its heartbreaking history, I didn't feel I could add to its future unless I could bring love back into these walls. I haven't felt that was a possibility until now."

That was probably one of the most sentimental and heartwarming things I had ever heard him say ... possibly even more than I have ever heard anyone say. The fact that he was bringing me there meant a lot. According to Colin, he felt he could breathe life and love into its walls with me by his side. His ability to expose the depths of his heart gave me yet another reason to fall deeper and deeper in love.

He lifted me in his arms as I clasped mine around his neck. He carried me through the grand entrance, and the sight inside was one to behold. It was pristine. It looked untouched but lived in at the same time. The interior was masterfully built and boasted natural wood from the surrounding area, slate harvested from the lake, and even driftwood from the shore. He put me down so I could explore. It was magnificent. It boasted three levels of living space, two turrets—one facing east and the other to the west—as well as a north-facing widow's walk. The latter, of which I'm sure, held nostalgic and poetic significance for the home.

Colin would explain that widow's walks were popular in 1800s New England. They served as an elevated vantage point for seamen's wives when they left for sea. Sadly, many never returned home. Colin's great-great-grandfather added the widow's walk while he served as a seafarer on Lake Erie. Although Lake Erie does not compare to the vastness of the sea, this large body of treacherous water had become the graveyard for many ships and their mates over the years. So, it was befitting for him to build it with the intention that his wife could count the sunrises and enjoy the sunsets while awaiting his return. Rich in history, it was truly an extraordinary feature. Unfortunately, Colin's great-great-grandfather never had the chance to move into the home. He met an untimely death on one of his seafaring adventures when the weather took a turn for the worse and capsized his boat. There he still lies among the crews of over 2,000 ships that have settled at the bottom of this treacherous Great Lake.

With every room, I was entranced by the beauty, elegance, and décor. And Colin was elated that I had taken such a liking to it. "How could one not?" I thought.

We spent a couple of hours admiring the exquisiteness of the home and the grounds that were equally as breathtaking. It was like being lost in a whole other world. "Someday," Colin said. "Someday," and he placed his arm around my shoulder as we stared out into our very own little sea.

We had so much to talk about the remainder of the way home. One of the highlights was that Colin had received his DNA testing kit. He had it all prepared and was planning on sending it back to the company in the morning mail. The real wait would begin, and for the next six weeks, I knew he'd be on edge.

With all the healthy discussion, I knew that Colin's focus had been to get my mind off of the boys' departure. I checked my watch and noted a text message from Devon letting me know that the boys had arrived and they were all safely back at home. I felt so much more at ease.

In the midst of all the jibber-jabber, we hadn't been paying much attention to our surroundings. Colin ended up driving right past the Duncan exit. Without thinking, we were headed in the direction of Ackerton. With that faux pas, we decided to continue on to check in with whatever part of the team was working. And, as it turned out, it was a good thing that we did.

We were greeted at the door by Chief Jeremy, who indicated that he was just getting ready to conference call Colin and me. He led us into the War Room, where several of the team members were already gathered. Chief Jeremy had called an emergency meeting. On a Sunday morning, it must have been important.

"The list is growing," he told the group.

There were about thirty-five more cases of missing persons and unsolved murders of young females, fitting our victim profile. These had occurred over the past nineteen years. The year 2005 seemed to be when they all started. These cases also fit the criteria of having occurred during the months of April through October, in areas within close proximity to university campuses. With the exception of some of the older unsolved crimes, nearly all victims were found somewhere along the banks of Lake Erie. With approximately 445 miles of mainland shoreline, he was living the dream on a huntsman's playground. Anywhere from one to three disappearances or murders had occurred within each given year, with the exception of a two- or three-year period where nothing occurred. This break would usually indicate some type of change in the suspect's life that would require him to pause his activities. Possibly a medical condition or accident of some sort.

The most interesting part of this list is that while the specificity of all dates could not be confirmed, it appeared that most had occurred on or around a full moon. And all victims were found with a red ribbon or red fabric fragments on or near their remains.

"Damn," I slipped as I spoke out loud.

We needed to bring more members onto our team; otherwise, it would take months upon months to scour through all these cases. We didn't have months. We had three more full moons left in this year that our suspect may view as opportunities to kill. We had three more full moons before he would go dormant for winter. We needed to find him, and we needed to find him now.

This led me to another chilling thought.

I looked at the group with a highly concerned expression and said out loud, "What *if* he was a snowbird? What *if* he had the capability to travel south for the winter?"

I shuddered to think.

CHAPTER 24

Special Delivery

Monday, September 2, 2024

The August full moon had come and gone. To our knowledge, there were no significant events that took place. No bodies were found ... all seemed quiet and still. Our investigation seemed to take on a snail's pace as well.

Taking advantage of the slower pace of the investigation, Colin and I decided to spend the Labor Day weekend camping. With the boys back in Virginia and Josie off to college, we enjoyed the long weekend tucked away in a rustic cabin in the woods ... just Colin and me.

It had been years since I had last gone camping. I had forgotten how much I enjoyed it. I can only blame myself for being so immersed in my work that I had forgotten what simple pleasures were made of.

Labor Day typically marked the beginning of cooler weather in Western New York, particularly in the evening. This was my favorite time to camp.

We spent most of our days enjoying nature on the hiking trails. We would set out early and witness the beauty of nature in all her glory. From the flittering wings of a tiny, little butterfly to the scampering feet of the frightened baby bunny, I was coming to appreciate the simpler sides of life. While learning to listen to my breath and feel the trail, I was becoming one with nature and finding a deeper self. By the end of the weekend, I felt as though I had woven myself into the landscape there ... a place where Colin and I had become the fabric of nature.

Completely surrounded by earthy notes that only a true forest can bring, nightfall would add a layer of warmth and nostalgia with the added scent of burning wood. As the smoke twirled above our heads, the flames flickered their dance and sent sparks of red snapping through the air. I could feel the warmth of the heat on my face as the low crackle hummed a comforting and calming tune. Curled in a blanket next to Colin, I was both mesmerized and entranced.

Colin had patiently reminded me how to take time to smell the flowers. Quite literally. I was grateful for the gentle reminder and for the chance to reset and recharge. Little did we know, however, this moment of calm was about to end.

I returned home to Mom's house late afternoon on Labor Day. Mom had gone out with her lady friends to the local Bingo Hall, so I had returned to an empty house. I entered the back door and tossed my keys in a little bowl on the counter as I did every day. As I did so, I noticed there was an envelope sitting next to the bowl, addressed to me.

"That seems odd," I thought to myself. "Why would I have mail, addressed to me, at my mother's house?"

I picked it up and made my way to the living room, where I sat down to open the mysterious delivery. Holding it out in front of me, I observed what looked like old-fashioned typing … like from a typewriter. There was no return address, and I wasn't familiar with the postmark.

"Now, this was really odd," I thought.

Sitting in the quiet of the dimly lit room, an eerie aura fell upon me. I had begun feeling anxious and hesitant; soon, I was fully aware of the pounding in my chest. I slowly opened the envelope.

Anticipating a letter of some sort, it appeared to have nothing inside. I pulled the envelope closer to my eyes, opened the sides wide, and peered in. I completely froze when I saw it.

"Is this some kind of sick joke?" I thought.

There it was. A delicate red ribbon tied in a nice neat bow. I gasped and instinctively turned to look behind me. I had a dreadful feeling like someone was standing there. Jumping to my feet and stumbling away from the chair, it appeared as though I was all alone. But that feeling of someone or something standing behind me lingered. I was completely freaked out.

I immediately reached for my cell phone. With my hands shaking, I speed-dialed Colin's number. By the time he answered, I was in a hysterical panic.

Colin came running to my rescue, along with several Duncan Police cars. Their three-minute response time seemed more like three hours as I stood among the creaking sounds of that old house. The neighbors were peering out their windows and were quick to wonder what all the commotion was about. One of them called my mom's cell phone and alerted her to the activity that was taking place. It wasn't long before she came rushing in.

"He knows where I live," I said to Colin. "How in the world does he know?"

"And why me? Did he taunt his other victims before he killed them? What am I missing?"

My eyes were pleading at Colin, searching for answers. But he had none. He could only offer his reassurance that he would not let anything happen to me. I knew, however, that he couldn't be with me at all

236

times. I also knew how this worked. Someone who has their mind set on doing harm will find a way to do it. Or, they will at least give it their best effort. My stomach was in knots.

I handed the envelope over to the police officer. I was doubtful that forensics would find very much, though. Our serial freak was too clever to leave any unwanted clues.

He clearly wanted me to know that he knew how to find me. "But why?" I thought. "Other than being part of the investigative team assigned to this case, what role did I play in his grand scheme?"

"It's all just a mind game," I told myself. "It's about getting into my head. He wants me to wonder if I'm next." The thought of this was unsettling for me. It would be unsettling for anyone ... no matter what their training or background was.

I needed to remain calm and think about this realistically. I wanted to be proactive, but I had to be analytical with how I viewed this situation. On one hand, I was of petite build. I had long dark hair, with highlights, albeit. I was of European descent. But that's where it ends. On the other hand, I was not a swimmer, and I was not a young, college-aged student. I wasn't particularly athletic looking, and I sported a small mommy pouch. If he was selectively picking me as a victim, he would have to change his entire pattern. His location, the scenario, how he lured his victims ... everything that took him years to develop would have to change. I could understand if he was evolving with the victim's age, but everything else considered, it just didn't paint a realistic picture of what may be going on here. I doubted he would easily give up what had taken years for him to perfect. So why me?

Then, I thought about Josie. Maybe through me, he found I have Josie. But I quickly dismissed this thought because Josie had left Mom's over a week ago and returned to college. She wasn't anywhere near Lake Erie, she wasn't a swimmer, and she didn't fit the victim M.O. A sense of relief washed over me. At the same time, I knew that I was the object of his eye. But again, "Why?"

The more I thought about it, the more I believed, "Maybe I'm a threat to him. Maybe I'm getting close. Just like he tried to throw me off the trail by pointing a finger at Fred, maybe he was trying to divert my attention elsewhere."

Colin's first instinct was to bring me and my mother to stay at his house. But Mom refused to go. She insisted that she was not going to let some deranged maniac scare her out of her own home. I, obviously, was not going to leave my mother in the house alone. So, Colin reverted to Plan B. He would stay here with Mom and me until he felt it was safe for us to be on our own again.

"Could I possibly love him any more than I already do?" I thought.

Mom was flustered by all the commotion, but I reassured her that we were dealing with someone who thrived on mind control. He wasn't likely to deviate too much from his normal patterns, so taunting me was just a game for him. Although I was not 100% convinced of this, I was at least somewhat successful in easing my mother's fears. In the back of my mind, though, I couldn't help but wonder if the other victims had received the same trinket in the mail. I could tell by the concerned look on Colin's face that he felt the same way too.

Mom was happy to have Colin in her home, even if it was under extenuating circumstances. It had been years since the scent of a man had walked among these walls. And, I had to admit, I was happy to have him here too.

As we all settled in for the night, Colin and I retreated to my bedroom. I lay close to him, snuggled up in his strong, masculine arms. I felt the warmth of his body shrouding me from the dangers of the outside world. I felt safe. But, as I slowly drifted off to sleep, I couldn't help but wonder …

"Was I next?"

CHAPTER 25

Final Plight

Wednesday, September 18, 2024

Last night, another full moon had fallen upon us. We had gotten word that another body was found in the early hours of this cool September morning. As soon as we heard the news, Colin and I were on our way to the scene of the crime.

About four hours west of Duncan lies the tiny little community of Emory Shores. Known for its sandy beaches and coastal cottages, this adorably quaint Michigan village is home to a mere 250 residents. The furthest thing from a touristy destination, Emory Shores is one of those forgotten little towns where peace and tranquility reside. The discovery of Georgia's lifeless body had shaken the community to its core.

By the time we arrived, it was late morning. Surrounded by a multitude of law enforcement vehicles, we approached the taped-off barrier. Looking ahead, I could see the body of a beautiful young woman, lying peacefully, on a cold gray slab of slate. The area was aloft with mumbling voices, camera flashes, and people in uniform pacing about. The news media was clamoring to get a closer view and attempting to solicit comments from the police.

Georgia had just turned twenty years old. Like the others, she was attending college and spent much of her time training at the nearby university swimming pool. Like the others, she was of petite build with broad shoulders. Her skin was pale against her long dark hair; her uncommon beauty was breathlessly captivating. If it weren't for her partially clad body, one might think she had simply fallen asleep.

I crouched down next to her. I closed my eyes, trying to hold back that one, lonely tear. But it was too late, and it was followed by more. I opened my eyes and stared down at the red ribbon tied delicately into a bow around her neck. This case was wearing on my heart. I felt responsible for this lifeless beauty lying before me because I hadn't been able to stop that maniac.

"I'm so sorry, Georgia. I'm so sorry that I didn't catch him before he caught you. Please forgive me," as I pushed back the tears.

And then, I recalled that our killer had a history of returning to the scene of the crime. I stood up and looked around. I would have surely noticed him had he been in the parking area where other onlookers were standing by.

"Where is he?" I thought.

I continued to scope out the area. The beach was dotted with wild shrubs and lush green trees. Sections of beach grass blew in the breeze. I peered through and around, up and down. And then, I saw him. There he was. Standing atop a cliff, close to the road. As soon as he knew he had garnered my attention, he turned away and disappeared.

"Did he leave? Or was he hiding in the trees?" I wondered.

"He's playing with me again," I thought. I quietly snuck away from the beach and headed toward the cliff where he had been standing. Following a path that meandered through the foliage, I wasn't afraid. I was pissed.

"If he wants me, he's going to get me," I thought to myself.

I drew my gun, elbows at my waist, arms bent straight up, holding my piece in front of my face. I took slow and steady steps as I approached the spot where he had been standing. I wasn't sure if he'd be there or not. As I reached the area, I stopped. I slowly exhaled as I extended my arms and held the gun out in front of me. I was ready to pull the trigger. But no one was there. He was gone.

I let out a sigh as I retracted my weapon. I reached for my cell phone and dialed Colin. He was shocked and upset that I had roamed off alone again. He would save his rant for later … when we were behind closed doors. For now, however, he sent some officers to my location to scour the area.

I couldn't believe it! "He was there … within our reach. And he simply slipped away."

I wondered, "How did he get away so quickly? Would there be any tracks for us to corroborate his vehicle?"

One of the responding officers approached me and asked for me to accompany him to the edge of the cliff. As I followed close behind, we stood at the opening where I had first seen our suspect. The officer pointed to a branch on a nearby bush. Attached to the branch with a red ribbon tied in a nice, neat bow was a typewritten note.

It said, "For you."

An arrow at the bottom of the note pointed directly to where the victim lay upon the beach. The reaction was instant. I turned and regurgitated what little I had eaten for breakfast. I was sickened and mortified.

Once my senses had returned, I apologized to the officer. I only wanted to know one thing at this point. "How was that bow tied?"

Without touching it, I carefully reviewed the direction of the fabric. It clearly appeared to be a left-handed bow. It also appeared to match the same bow I had received in the mail. As it turned out, the latter had been tied by a left-hand-dominant individual as well.

"Mind games," I was sure of it.

Needless to say, the ride home was a long one. Colin's rant lasted longer than the one he had when I had run off and met with Fred. But again, I knew his anger was coming from a place of love.

"I can't help it, Colin. I acted on instinct. When I saw him, I only knew I had to reach him. I wasn't thinking of me or my own safety. I couldn't save Georgia, so I was thinking about saving someone else ... the next girl," I explained.

"I get it, Sonny. I really do. And you've done well for all these years without me harping on you. But I can't help it either. I lost you once. I just can't do it again."

I realized I was going to have to learn to hold myself back. I acknowledged to him that I would work on developing more restraint. Especially when it came to my safety. It never is a good idea to go off alone into unknown territory. I learned that as far back as when I was a Brownie, when they introduced me to the Buddy System. I knew better.

We were halfway back to Duncan when Colin pulled off the highway. I asked where he was going, and he said, "You'll see."

The winding road was lined on both sides with tall, majestic oak trees. Branching out over the road from either side, we were trekking through a tunnel of green. It was absolutely stunning, and coming out the other end, a rundown old shanty came into view. It certainly wasn't anything spectacular, and it was in dire need of a new coat of paint. It seemed lost out there ... so out of place.

As Colin pulled closer to the building, a flashing sign above the door came into view. *The Outpost*, it read, as it flickered on and off.

"What in the world is this, Colin?" I asked.

He chuckled and said, "Only the best barbeque you will ever taste in your life."

And he was absolutely right! This little off-the-beaten-path restaurant may not have looked like much, but it served up a feast that was finger-licking good! It was so satiating, we left with full bellies and the promise to return. We were both exhausted after all the food we ate and were glad to arrive home before nightfall.

Mom was sitting in her favorite chair reading a book. She loved to read. As I walked in, she looked up above her glasses and said, "You've got more mail."

"What?" I exclaimed.

"It's on the coffee table in front of the couch," she said.

My eyes shifted toward the coffee table. There it was. A familiar envelope with the same familiar typed address on it. And sure enough, there was my name. It held no return address, and the postmark? There was no postmark.

"Oh my gosh. He's getting scarily brave. Did he bring this to our house? Was he here?" Millions of questions were going through my mind.

I could feel knots building in my stomach. The tightness was mounting as Colin looked at me. "Do you want me to open it, Sonny?"

"No! I've got this!" as I tore open the top.

I looked inside. This time there was a letter. Part of me dreaded opening it; the other part was hoping it might unearth some type of clue. But, as I unfolded the paper that I held inside my hands, the words came into view. They were written in the same typed lettering that the envelope sported. With Colin at my side and my mother looking on, I read it out loud:

"I know why you hunt me,

just know I hunt you too.

My dearest, darling Sonny,

soon enough, I'll be with you.

I hide in the shadows of the night,

I'm the dawning of each new day.

This will be my final plight,

to take your breath away."

"He's crazy!" I screamed! "He's absolutely crazy! I'm not even his type! Am I?"

I instantly started barking out commands.

"I want someone following up to see if the other victims received messages."

"I want all the neighborhood video cams checked for this psycho."

"I want this letter gone through with a fine-tooth comb!"

"I want a name, dammit! I want a name!"

Colin was deeply disturbed. He did his best to calm me down. He insisted that he was going to have a police officer posted outside my mother's house 24/7 until the perpetrator was caught.

As far as I was concerned, all logic was out the door. I had my answer now.

He was coming for me.

CHAPTER 26

The Red Wolf

Fast forward to October. It was a day like any other day at the office. Things had been fairly quiet since I had received that mysterious poem. There were no major developments in finding our perpetrator. No prints had been found on the envelope. Neighborhood videos hadn't turned up any credible evidence. Either the images were not clear, or follow-up on vehicular and pedestrian traffic offered no leads. Law enforcement had determined that the individual who delivered the envelope may have come through the backyards. A scour of video cams around the block was of no help either. It was rather disappointing. Something had to give. I felt like we were running out of time. If all my estimations were correct, the final full moon of his killing season would be upon us. I was worried.

Would he come for me?

Would he take a new victim?

Would he do nothing?

All three scenarios were distressing. The first two for obvious reasons. In the latter, I feared we would lose him while he hibernated for the winter, and then we would have to start tracking all over again in the spring.

I had awoken this particular morning, absent of wakefulness, due to the interrupted sleep the night before. My body and brain had easily fallen into a deep slumber. It was the first of many nights that I would fall limp before midnight. But it seemed that just as quickly as I had fallen asleep, I would be awakened again. I had opened my groggy eyes in the vastness of the dark room. Though I could not see, I had the distinct sensation that I was not alone.

Knowing Colin should be lying next to me, I reached over to make sure he was still there. He was there, fast asleep. I placed my hand on his forearm and gently shook him. His only reaction was to let out a little groan and turn away from me onto his side.

Squinting through the darkness, my vision was obscured by the shadows. I sat up in my bed searching and calling out.

"Is anybody there?"

Looking toward the foot of my bed, I continued to strain in an effort to focus my eyesight on the presence I had been feeling.

Slowly, the outline of a human figure began to take form. I should have been terrified to see someone standing before me, in the middle of the night, invading the safety of my bedroom ... especially under the threat of our serial killer. But for some reason, I wasn't afraid. Maybe it was Colin's slumber presence, or maybe it was something more. Something I couldn't explain.

Reaching out toward the figure, it soon became clear. I gasped.

It was Anna!

A sense of calmness filled the entire space. It was a feeling unlike any I had felt before. Radiantly clothed, her delicate white dress flowed softly to her knees as she outstretched both of her arms to me. I was immediately drawn to her embrace. Our lips did not move; not a word was spoken. Yet in the quietness of the room, we shared an entire conversation.

It was the most spiritual and powerful experience I had ever had. When I awoke the next morning, I was still accompanied by the same sense of peace. And how was it that Colin should lie right next to me and never be stirred? He was completely oblivious.

"Was it all just a dream?" I asked myself.

Our encounter was one that had been far more vivid than your average dream. It seemed so real. It was difficult to digest that we had an entire conversation with unspoken words, yet I understood everything that was said. It was the strangest experience, and upon awakening, I could no longer recall the specifics of our dialogue. Although I remembered no specific words, I was left with a feeling that everything was going to be just fine. I felt such a sense of peace.

I needed that affirmation. The affirmation of peace. Because the deeper I dove into this investigation, the more I was haunted. Not only was I haunted by the cries of the dead, but also now by threats that I may be next.

As I continued to think about what had happened, I recalled something she said. "Relax. Just breathe. Breathe for you, and then breathe for me."

"What was Anna telling me?" I thought. Little did I realize, the intent of this statement was a hugely powerful one. One that would soon be revealed.

Slowly, additional details began to fade in. First was an odd detail, but one that I'm sure held some type of significance. Before Anna had departed from my dream, she had shown me a red wolf. Of average size, its thick coat of fur was mostly unkempt. It had a long bushy tail, which is what separated its breed from that of your everyday, common dog. I thought the deep red coloring was a bit odd for a wolf, but what did I really know about wolves anyway? Its eyes were set deep in its forehead; they were hollow and black.

At that moment, I experienced déjà vu, recalling the red wolf that appeared in my dreams back in 2004. Why is it that I would now have recollections of a dream that occurred the night before my own rape? I really wasn't sure what it all meant, but I felt a negative aura, and it certainly didn't leave me with a warm and fuzzy feeling.

As a final detail emerged, I recalled that Anna held a glass of deep red wine in one hand. In the other, she held a strand of grapes. Everyone knew Anna was a huge connoisseur of fine wines, so it didn't seem out of place that she would appear with them. While I'm sure there was a deeper underlying meaning, I failed to understand what it was.

"Anna ... a red wolf ... and a glass of red wine." I thought. "How are these all connected?" Still pondering the validity of the dream, I was truly baffled. Mostly, by the significance of the *red wolf*. This aspect of the dream deeply disturbed me.

I had plans later that evening with Lydia and the girls. Lydia invited us all over for some eats, drinks, and healthy conversation, as she called it. I hadn't seen them since Anna's funeral luncheon, and I was looking forward to having some much-needed girl time.

I was a tad late arriving at Lydia's. The girls were gathered around the island table chatting and laughing. Lydia had made quite the spread of hors d'oeuvres … shrimp cocktail, spinach artichoke dip, seafood pizza, buffalo chicken wings, beef on weck sliders, and the list went on and on. That was Lydia, always outdoing herself. I noticed the half-filled glass of wine sitting on the counter. It sat in front of an empty stool; no one was drinking from it.

Jenn had taken notice of my observation and said, "It's for Anna … her favorite wine." She smiled.

It wasn't long before we were all reminiscing about Anna. Bantering back and forth with a few laughs and a few more tears. I thought I might use this as an opportunity to mention my dream. So, as we sat around talking, I shared my experience.

Ironically, each of the other girls had similar stories. All were visited at night by Anna, who was standing at the base of their beds. All being comforted in her warm embrace and having entire conversations without ever moving their lips. She came to each in a very vivid dream. Although the messages were different, the similarity of her visits was uncanny.

My dream, however, was unique in that she showed me a *red wolf*. When I mentioned this to them, they had no idea what it could have possibly meant. Although we threw various ideas around, we were all stumped. One thing we did agree on, though, was that these experiences were more than just ordinary dreams. We were all convinced that they were *visitation dreams,* where Anna actually visited each of us. This is one of those situations where if you hadn't experienced it for yourself, you'd likely think it wasn't true. The fact that we all had a similar experience, unbeknownst to each other, told me there was something to it and that *something* just couldn't be explained.

Moving along in conversation, we all had a lot of catching up to do. Lydia gave an update on all the creative things she was making. If it wasn't a mosaic wall hanging filled with beach glass in varying shades, along with a multitude of other artist media, then she was onto some type of sewing project. Everything Lydia touched turned to gold, and her creations were in high demand.

Emily was busy talking about *her* version of Fred's arrest. While she strategically left out some of the juicier details of the case, she told how this ordeal had made her marriage stronger. I wasn't sold on the idea. On the outside, I acted excited for her. But on the inside, I had no respect for Fred ... especially after his attempts at holding my hand.

Then there was Jenn ... the perpetual flower child of the group. She spoke of her children a lot. She was very proud of her kids. She was completely clueless when it came to the world around her, but she did talk about her garden. She spent a considerable amount of time discussing her attempts at crossbreeding some of her organic vegetables. I didn't understand any of it, so she lost my attention early on during that part of the conversation.

Then, it was my turn. I talked about my visit with the kids and how they enjoyed being in Duncan. I updated them about my mother. But I was saving the juiciest details for last. So finally, I just blurted it out. "Colin and I are back together again!"

The excitement among the three was no surprise. They wanted to know every smutty little detail. It seemed not much had changed in the past twenty years when it came to new romances in our lives. We were expected to share the hot and juicy details about our new loves so the others, who were leading boring lives, could live vicariously. Girl code, I guess. Of course, however, I had my pride. So, I remained guarded over the information I shared. What I did divulge seemed to be enough to satisfy their interest. Of this, I was glad.

Anna's half-filled glass of wine garnered my attention again. This time I noticed the bottle sitting next to it. In big bold letters I read, "Perricone."

I grasped the bottle, and while holding it in my hand, I stared down at the letters. "Perricone," I said slowly. "Perricone," I repeated in a more natural tone. "Perricone," I said once again. It sounded so familiar.

"That's it!" I exclaimed out loud!

The girls all looked at me in astonishment. I had startled them. "What's it?" asked Emily.

I caught myself. I didn't want to disclose anything from the case. "Oh, nothing. Just a random thought that I had. I have random thoughts all the time," and I laughed it off.

But it was far from funny. I continued to hold the bottle, gaping down at the label. Perricone happened to be a rare, red-wine grape. It was used in the manufacture of *specialty* wines. The label told of a grape, primarily harvested in the Sicily region of Italy, that gave the wine its texture and deep red pigment. This was Anna's favorite. But it was also something else. I knew why it sounded so familiar.

Perricone was also a lesser-known pharmaceutical company. I had come across them before, in another case. With headquarters in Idaho, they dealt in the manufacture and sale of what they referred to as *specialty* drugs. "And, that was it!!" I thought excitedly! I excused myself to step out and make a call.

257

I called the Ackerton Police Department and found Chief Jeremy was still there. He had teams working around the clock researching, analyzing, and investigating every possible angle. With him on the line, I said, "It's Perricone. I think our perp may be working for Perricone Pharmaceuticals."

Chief Jeremy knew not to ask me *why*. He knew only to trust my instinct. And with that, he said he'd follow up with the lead. I took in a deep breath and slowly released it. I knew I had something there. I just knew it.

"Thank you, Anna," I said in a whisper, and turned the handle on the door.

I returned to the girls with a sense of triumph. There they stood, outside the glass patio doors, arm in arm as they stared out at the cascading waves. My senses were surrounded by the sound of rushing water as it gently crashed to shore. I joined in their embrace. With the passing of September, summer had officially ended. The air had become cooler, and leaves were taking on new form before they would soon fall from their limbs. The four of us would have few opportunities to enjoy this breathtaking view together before winter would roll in.

As the evening grew darker, the angled rays of the sun cast hues of red and orange throughout the sky. The warm tinge of amber light set the sky ablaze in color. Silently together, we enjoyed this passive and peaceful moment.

Little did I know, however, this was the calm before the chaos.

CHAPTER 27

Hunter's Moon

Thursday, October 17, 2024

As the crisp autumn air descended upon the small town of Duncan, leaves had changed to shades of fiery red, golden yellow, and sunset orange. The second week of October always brought together the height of colors in a stunning display of nature's beauty. The vibrancy of Western New York's fall foliage was the only thing that rivaled the Lake Erie sunsets.

I had just finished a quick morning run when Colin pulled into my mother's driveway. He was returning from an early morning appointment at the gym. "Good morning, Love!" I said as I greeted him with a kiss.

"It's an outstanding morning, Sonny!" Colin seemed much more jovial than usual.

I looked at him with a confused look as he took me by my hand and led me over to the front stoop. He sat me down as he pulled his cell phone from the front pocket of his athletic pants.

As he scrolled over the top of his screen, he asked, "Are you ready?"

"Ready? Ready for what?" I asked.

"Um, only for the best day ever!" he exclaimed.

Now he **really** had piqued my curiosity. I had no idea what he was talking about. "The best day ever?" I knew that could mean a whole lot of things.

Squinting at his screen, Colin proceeded to read, "50% shared deoxyribonucleic acid. Parent/Child."

I don't know where my train of thought was, but still, I was at a loss. Looking at him inquisitively, I had no idea what he was talking about.

"The DNA test, Sonny! I'm her father! I'm Josie's father!!!"

Shivers of goosebumps ran up and down every extremity I had. They even ran up and down ones I didn't have. I couldn't believe my ears.

"What?" I asked as I looked at Colin in both shock and dismay.

Tears welled up in my eyes. Tears of joy. It was exactly as Colin had expected. He knew. He knew all along. There is something to be said about that natural parental bond. I should have trusted his instinct.

He held his phone in my direction to bring the results into view, and, sure enough, there was a parent and child relationship noted between Colin and my daughter with the fictitious name. I bolted to my feet and flung my arms around his neck!

"Oh, Colin! This **IS** the best day ever!"

We lingered in our embrace.

Years of being followed by a hovering gray cloud had lifted. I finally felt that I could leave the fateful day in May 2004 behind. But now I had reached a whole new level of regret. I had cheated Josie and Colin out of nineteen years of their lives … nineteen years of bonding and the opportunity to form a father-daughter relationship. More tears welled up in my eyes, but now for another reason. I soon burst into tears and shared my regret with Colin. But, in Colin's true fashion, he comforted me. He assured me that there was no room for regret.

Everything was exactly as it should be. Everything happens for a reason. He reminded me that had we known from the start that Josie was his, the trajectory of my whole life would be different. I would never have joined the military. I would not have met my husband and had my boys. I wouldn't be working in the field I was in.

He said, "And who knows, instead of falling in love all over again, we might be hating each other right now."

I knew that he was right.

Contemplating what I might say to my mother, I wanted Colin by my side when I delivered the news. So, although I knew he was not a fan of breakfast, I asked him to join us anyway. He looked at me with a side-eyed grin. He knew where this was going.

"You want me to delay my shower?" he asked.

With a pleading look in my eyes, he placed his hand on mine and gave it a little squeeze. It was clear he understood my intentions; there was no fooling him.

"Well, I suppose I could go for some scrambled eggs this morning," he said.

Before we went inside, Colin inquired what my mother has thought all these years regarding the identity of Josie's father. I told him that my explanation to her was that Josie's conception was born out of an ill-fated union.

263

I continued, "I told her pretty much the same as I had always told Josie. It didn't matter how she was conceived; it only mattered that she was born."

I further explained that as far as they were concerned, her conception may have resulted from a one-night stand. No matter what they believed, however, it was an unspoken truth that the man who fathered Josie would not be a figure in her life. Both my mom and Josie accepted that and respected me enough never to question any of the details.

Mom had made quite the morning spread. Easy over eggs with bacon and sausage, homemade pancakes with syrup right from the tree, and fresh-squeezed orange juice were all intricately placed on the table ready for us to enjoy. I kidded with her and suggested that the only thing missing was the milk, straight from the cow.

Colin kidded her too, "What? No scrambled eggs?"

We all chuckled together, which served to lighten the mood. I thought this would be a good lead-in for our news.

I asked Mom to sit down. She was both curious and wary. "We have some news, Mom."

Immediately, she said, "You're pregnant!"

I let out a little laugh. "Why would that be the first thing you think of?" I asked.

As she shrugged her shoulders, I assured her I was not pregnant. But I told her she wasn't completely out in left field either. I proceeded to share our news about Josie and Colin. Not surprisingly, she was happily astonished.

"Come to think of it, she has your eyes," she said as she looked in Colin's direction.

She was right. Josie **did** have his eyes. And the more I looked at him, the more I saw my daughter … the daughter that for so many years I thought had been born out of tragedy, but who had actually been born out of love. It was impossible to describe what I was feeling at that moment. Piece by piece, it seemed as though my life was finally coming together.

As for Josie? I don't think there were words that could even begin to describe how I believed she would feel. I did know, however, that she would be elated. She would finally have the biological father that she so desperately wanted. And, seeing how she and Colin got along, I don't think she could have picked a better one if she tried. I couldn't wait to tell my sweet, loving Josie.

All the swirling emotions had caused an obvious morning distraction that slowed down my regular routine. With the last gulp of juice and realizing the time, Colin and I did a mad dash, racing to see who could get to the shower first. I won. Soon enough, though, we were out the door, ready for a brand-new day.

We arrived at the Ackerton PD just after 10 a.m. As we approached the doors of the station, we were immediately surrounded by a multitude of news outlets clamoring for a statement. Squeezing past them and through the door, the interior halls were equally filled with a sense of commotion.

"What in the world was all this brouhaha about?" I asked Colin.

Not necessarily expecting an answer, he shrugged his shoulders as we headed straight for Chief Jeremy's office. Once safely inside, Chief Jeremy shut the door and turned with a smile.

"We got him," he said. "We got the bastard!"

"What? How? Who?" I stammered.

Chief Jeremy looked at Colin and me. "We got our killer, Sonny."

"We've got a name. We've got a location. He actually only lives about thirty miles south of here. Our guys are on their way now to pick him up," he said as he continued.

"And it's thanks to you, Sonny. I don't know how you did it. And I don't care. But you did it."

I stood there, mouth gaping open wide. "Me?" I asked.

"You, Sonny. You and your crazy, sensational, analytical mind."

As it turned out, the tip I gave to Chief Jeremy, about Perricone, panned out. He had immediately followed up on it, obtaining a court order to garner their list of employees. Each one had been issued an identification badge. With that list came badge information, including photos. Our team was able to match the suspect's photo with one of the badges. Once we had his name, everything fell into place.

Chief Jeremy continued his brag. He specifically pointed out that my probing nature led to the discovery of Anna's phone, which proved to be a vital piece of information and evidence. He also professed that my inquiring mind caused them to expand their investigation over a longer period of time and into a larger geographical region. It was a direction that they would never have thought of, but a direction that was proving to be true. With each new path that I suggested, more clues and details would emerge. He felt genuinely confident that it was my ability to interpret the evidence that allowed me to guide the team.

His words, "With each new and invaluable piece of information, no matter how small, you were able to unweave the tangled web, piece by piece."

I got it. I understood what he was saying, and I was flattered. I knew how important profiling was to any investigation, which is why I chose this as my profession. But I knew that I had a helper. Her name was Anna. And I also knew that it took an entire team, not just one person. We each brought our own unique expertise to the table. Through a unified approach, **WE** did this! We did it together!

Chief Jeremy asked Colin and me to join him at the podium they were preparing outside. He was going to be releasing a public statement, and he wanted us available to answer questions. Just as we both agreed to join him, he received a call. And following a brief conversation, he hung it up.

Grinning from ear to ear, "They got him! They've got him in custody!"

Chief Jeremy continued, "They caught him at home just as he was on his way out the door. He had his car all packed with his tools of the trade … red ribbon, needles, syringes, and vecuronium. He had every intention of striking again. Your tip on Perricone was the break we needed. It saved a life today, Sonya! Maybe even your own!"

A sense of overwhelming relief enveloped me. This sickening animal had intended one last hurrah in our region before the weather turned too cold. At tonight's full moon, he would kill one more time. His words reverberated inside me. *"This will be my final plight, to take your breath away."* The reality of the moment sent a chill up and down my spine.

Contemplating this, I realized the irony of his plan. During my extensive research, I had learned there were different names given to the full moons in each month. October's full moon was referred to as the *Hunter's Moon*. It was traditionally known as the full moon that marks the beginning of hunting season. It calls on hunters to take advantage of the moon's illumination when tracking their prey.

After this day, however, the October full moon would take on a whole new meaning. Our perp would no longer track … he would no longer prey. This full moon would signify that **HIS** hunt was over and …

… so, mine would be too.

With a bold confidence and sense of liberation, we stepped out into the ceaseless clicking of cameras and the blinding flashes of light.

It was time for us to write the end of this horrid story.

A time for us to offer renewed hope to the communities that had been so severely affected.

And it was a time to breathe new life into new beginnings.

After today, I had only *one* thing left to do.

CHAPTER 28

Interview With Satan

Not how I would have chosen to spend my weekend, but due to scheduling and coverage issues, I was at the mercy of the maximum-security Pennsylvania State Prison facility where our suspect was being held. Although it was a several-hour drive for me, I was okay with that. Colin wanted to accompany me, but I knew this was something I needed to confront on my own. The drive there would give me some quiet time to mentally prepare for what I was about to face.

November 2nd. All Soul's Day. How ironic that this would be the day I visited the devil. In my Christian faith, All Soul's Day is a day of prayer and remembrance for the faithfully departed. What better day to honor those who lost their lives at his merciless hands? A fitting day to confront him, in an attempt to find some semblance of closure and peace for his victims.

As the correction officers escorted me down the long, dark hallway, I could hear the echo of every footstep we took. With each step I was acutely aware of the other sounds that surrounded me—metal scraping metal, doors clanking open and shut, and locks bolting behind me. A persistent musty odor permeated every breath. Until finally, we stood before a huge steel door. I shuddered for a moment in the bitter cold air. Lying beyond that door, just steps away, I would come face to face with pure evil. His name was Satanás Rojas Ochoa. By the community, he had become known as the Red Ribbon Strangler. To his inner circle, he was called Satan.

The door slowly opened. There he was, sitting before me with a smug grin on his face. The room was damp and cold. The familiar feeling of dread came over me, like a protective voice that tries to warn me when something bad is about to happen. I knew I didn't need to fear harm within these walls, but I still couldn't shake that foreboding feeling. And just as quickly as that feeling came along, it was replaced with a warm wave of comfort that had washed over me. I felt as though Anna was right there next to me … holding my hand.

I breathed a sigh of relief. Seeing him locked up in jail, bound with chains and shackles, was surreal. I looked around. Three officers guarded the door. There were no windows to allow the light of day to enter.

I thought to myself, "This is exactly where he is supposed to be ... locked away, like the animal he is, where he will never again see the light of day." It made me nauseous to even look at him.

"Remember me?" he said with a smirk, as he appeared to be looking right through me.

A shiver went up my spine, but I looked at him, unamused. "I **did** remember him. I could not forget those eyes." This was the same man that approached me at Anna's luncheon following her funeral. The man who tried to lead me to believe that Anna's secret "lover" was her killer. He was the unknown at the celebration of her life … mockingly toying with me, right in plain sight. He was also the same man who revisited the crime scenes and appeared in the photos. The same one who fled the scene of his last kill in Michigan after he garnered my attention. And the one who sent the red ribbon and delivered the poem to my house.

"How had he known to approach **me**? How did he know my name when he addressed the poem? Had he known me all along?" I was completely creeped out.

I continued to stare intently, not reacting to his gaze or his comment. We had already learned so much about him, but I would need to maintain my composure in order to get the last of my questions answered.

"Tell me about the Red Wolf." I said with an air of confidence.

I really didn't expect a response. It was a detail of my dream that had still bothered me, so I thought I would take a chance to see if it meant anything to him. To my surprise, he responded.

"It's me," he said. "My name."

He continued. "Rojas means 'red.' Ochoa means 'wolf.' Ironically, my first kill occurred on the eve of the Wolf Moon, January's full moon. I identify closely with the red wolf. How do you know about it? It's nothing I've ever shared."

I didn't respond. I now knew that this is what Anna had been trying to tell me. She wanted me to find the *Red Wolf*. And now that we had, things were coming together, and it all made perfect sense.

We had learned that Satanás was, in fact, a snowbird after all. Against our deepest fears, he actually started his killing spree down south during the winter months. This would account for, as he said, his first kill during the month of January in 2005.

"That was the year Josie was born," I thought to myself. "His first kill was only a month before."

A profound sadness came over me as I lamented the realization that these victims were young girls, just like my Josie. Each of them was someone's daughter, sister, granddaughter, or friend. His ability to travel according to the seasons had served to widen the kill zone and increase his number of prey. With the exception of some of his earlier kills, all were found near bodies of water; the full moons with their gravitational pull and effect on the tides proved to be important too. It all became part of his story to lure his victims to the location where they would die. It was his excuse to test their stamina as part of the evaluation for their acceptance into his fictitious swim camp. Little did they know that swimming in the higher tide would also serve to weaken their ability to fight back before their demise.

Satanás Rojas Ochoa was a sixty-two-year-old male of Spanish descent. He stood at about 5'10" tall with a thin build. His age was emphasized by the silvery highlights of his stringy mange as it sat disheveled upon his rounded shoulders. Far from clean-shaven, he presented with a soiled appearance. Underneath the shadowy growth, deep creases lined his face, making him look much older than he actually was. And those eyes … his eyes were filled with pure evil. It was so clear now. One could drown, gasping for air, in the depth of darkness he harbored within.

After our initial encounter, Satanás' cocky exterior softened. He became more relaxed and pleasant and was only too happy to boast of his conquests. With the exception of those sinister eyes, I completely understood his convincing appeal. It was as if he had transformed into a completely different person right before my eyes. His easy smile projected a friendly demeanor, and his sales pitch was well-versed and convincing.

Since his arrest, Satanás had confessed to a total of seventy-eight rapes and murders that spanned a nineteen-year period. Sixty-four of those confessions had been undisputably matched to victims through mostly physical, but in some cases, DNA evidence. With his photographic memory, he was able to accurately describe what his victims looked like as well as where and how he killed them. It was through his confession that police were able to solve so many missing person cases and recover their bodies. Considering that this was a capital case involving a wide range of jurisdictions, it was pretty evident that he would be looking at the death penalty. That day couldn't come soon enough.

We had learned that Satanás had been sexually abused throughout his youth, sometimes having been violently accosted. His mother, whose primary role in life was to support her drug habit through prostitution, was known to loan or rent Satanás out for favors. He developed a deep resentment for his mother and toward those, primarily women, who abused him. One such woman, Susan, was particularly heinous toward him. This would explain his repeated calling out of her name on the recording from Anna's phone.

In response to these young experiences, Satanás viewed women, in general, as overly sexual. This angered him. But even with his mother's abusive and neglectful role in his life, he held conflicting emotions toward her ... jumping to her defense at the mere suggestion that she might have been inept. Satanás' father played a nonexistent role in his life. He met him on two occasions, both of which his father completely denied paternity and ignored him. Devastated by his insignificant existence and invisibility to his father, Satanás developed a violent and explosive personality.

Satanás was married at the time of his arrest. In an interview, his wife described him as emotionally detached and cold on most occasions. She indicated that he would express his pain and resentment through acts of violence toward her. At other times, however, he would become every woman's dream, behaving like a loving and doting husband. That was the Satanás who captured her heart.

Intimately, she described their relationship as one in which they found mutual enjoyment in rough sex. Sometimes, it got to the point that he was provoked into a physical attack, after which, both enjoyed intense pleasures. In all encounters, she was expected to react submissively to his advances. The parallels between his relationship with his wife and his behavior in the act of rape-murder were uncanny. The biggest difference, however, was that in the latter, he was actually able to take his sadistic fantasies to the next level. His signature rape-violence had become a gross reiteration of the sexual performance he invoked from his wife.

Satanás hadn't always targeted his victims specifically from university swim facilities. Initially he began by prowling campus towns, after dusk, for vulnerable targets. The victims selected throughout his entire rape-murder career all bore similar physical features; those features, we learned, were rooted in his mother's identity. His internal conflicts about his mother played a critical role in his behavior and helped form his views of women as sexual pigs. This haunted his thoughts and fed his deepest resentments.

As time went on, his targets became more selective, and he began to engage in stalking activities. Each new tweak to his pattern was meant to add to the excitement and create an additional challenge. After an unfortunate event resulted in a severe back injury, he would be forced to take a break from his spree. But when he came back, he came back with a vengeance, and his behavior would evolve into what it has become today—a complex web of plots and lies. The three things that remained consistent, however, were the physical features of his preferred victims, his method of killing, and his signature red ribbon. In nearly every case, a red ribbon had been found on or near the victim; in those few cases that one was not found, mostly due to the age of some of the remains that had been recovered, red fibers consistent with the ribbon were present.

In filling in the gaps, Satanás explained about his vehicle. A parallel to my original theory, he had rebuilt the vehicle from a salvaged title many years prior. This would enable him to slide it under the radar of legal authorities. Using a recycled license plate, it was meant to mimic the vehicle he had been driving during his first attack. As a former truck driver, he owned a semi and had maintained his commercial driver's license, so he was able to load his vehicle into the back and transport it undetected. He only brought it out of hiding on the days he would commit his crimes.

As a profiler, part of my passion lies in the understanding of why people do what they do. But in this case, there was no rationale. Still, I looked at him directly in the eyes and asked, "What made you pick the girl from Duncan? She was much older than the others. Why her?"

"Aw, her? She was a mistake." He made a gesture like it was no big deal.

"I didn't realize her age until we were up close and talking. That's when she revealed that she wasn't a student. By then, I had too much invested in selecting her. It kind of grossed me out; hers wasn't as perky and tight. But I banged her just the same as all the others. And she liked it. I could see it in her eyes."

I looked at him with hate-filled eyes. As disgust welled up in my throat, I said, "Well, you know, Satanás, *that mistake* is what ultimately cost you your freedom!"

279

The room felt strangely lighter, as if Anna's spirit had again passed through. I knew he felt it too, as he let out an obvious, visible shiver.

"Your current job as a pharmaceutical sales rep gave you access to the vecuronium; how were you able to take it and remain undetected?" I asked.

"Perricone had no idea how many samples I actually gave away. I kept half for myself," he said.

"You know, I tried it out on my wife the first time. She was NOT happy with me," as he let out a little chuckle.

I felt nothing but utter disdain. I couldn't imagine that she would be amused, even to the slightest degree. But this behavior demonstrated the type of sick mind we were dealing with. He explained that he hadn't considered how quickly the drug might leave the body but added, "Pretty ingenious, wasn't that?" Satanás looked masterfully glib.

I responded, "Not impressive, and far from unique." I wasn't going to give him any satisfaction.

"I wished I had the vecuronium for my first victim though. Now **she** was a feisty one."

"Tell me about her," I said, still trying to understand what made him tick.

"Ohhhhh, she was special." He let out a little groan and leaned forward, placing his elbows on the table. Staring into my eyes, he slowly ran his tongue over his top lip in a disgusting attempt to appear sensual. He spoke slowly with much inflection as he articulated, "It was the most *explosive … sexually erotic … experience … I had ever had in my life!*"

"She wasn't part of the victim count, you know," he continued.

He had piqued my interest. "Why not?" I asked, in surprise. "Why would you not claim your first, most impactful conquest? And why the red ribbon?" I asked.

"The thrill of my first time is indescribable. I have never been able to get her salty, yet oh-so-savory, flavor from my mouth. Not even after twenty years." He continued as a grotesque slurp escaped his lips.

"Twenty years?" I thought to myself. I knew his first kill dated back nineteen years. I wondered how many other victims there were that we didn't know about.

"And to answer your last question … the ribbon. I found a red ribbon on the seat of my car that night. She had left behind a trophy … a trophy that I carried with me each time I took a life. It was my personal reminder *never* to screw up again."

He paused as he grew more agitated and shifted in his chair.

"And, after I squeezed the life out of each of them, one by one, I left a trophy too … a single red ribbon to mark my territory and denote victory.

"Sick F$%k," I thought to myself. I did my best not to show a reaction as I spoke, "Oh, but you did screw up, Satanás. You screwed up a lot."

Unfazed by my comment, he said, "You know, you look a lot like her." He closed his eyes and smiled a satisfying grin.

I realized at this point that he had begun to undress me with his eyes and in his mind. The mere recollection of this memory was turning him on.

I knew I needed to redirect the conversation, but I still wanted to know more about this new victim. "How exactly did you screw up?" I asked.

His eyes were piercingly cold as they stared at me. He held his eerie gaze. I tilted my head to the right and raised my eyebrows inquisitively. He spoke slowly and steadily.

"She was the *only one* who ever got away."

He was staring at me with a scrutiny that pierced my soul. And suddenly, it struck me! I knew where I'd seen those eyes before.

In an instant, I could feel my world collapsing around me. Like bricks in a wall, falling to the ground, one by one … landing on top of me and smothering the very air I breathed. I could feel the color escape my cheeks as my heart began to pound incessantly. I felt a squeezing in my chest … tighter and tighter … as I collapsed to the floor. All the while, I wondered why all these girls had to die. The prison guard rushed to my side. In pure panic, I could hardly breathe.

Satan looked on with a satisfying grin; he was completely enamored by his perceived success. His smugness wasn't just a matter of pathological pride; he was enjoying this moment of neurotic control. The other guards immediately grabbed hold of him and shuffled him toward the door.

In the back of my mind I could hear, "Sonny … "

"Relax. Just breathe. Breathe for you, and then breathe for me."

It was Anna.

I took her advice. I paused and took a deep breath in. I exhaled and took another. I was finally able to catch my breath … My eyes were pleading, "Why," as they trailed behind him exiting the door.

And all the while, I had become acutely aware …

… I was the one who got away!

CHAPTER 29

The Final Chapter

Saturday, November 2, 2024

There was no way I could let it end that way. If he walked away seeing me in that state, then he would have won. He would have claimed me for his victim … again. As I regained my composure, the guard helped me to my feet. I brushed myself off and looked him straight in the eye.

"I want him brought back in!" I said in a firm and confident tone.

The guard looked at me like I was crazy as he said, "You what? Are you sure?"

"I'm sure," I insisted. "I'm 100% sure!"

I felt overcome by a new sense of strength. I promised myself that if I ever had the chance to meet him face-to-face, it would be different than the last time. I would be strong. I would be the one in control. I would not be afraid. This was my chance, and although I had a moment of weakness, that's all it was … just a moment. I wanted him to know *who* was in charge now and *who* was silencing *him* once and for all.

As the guard called on his walkie-talkie to bring Satanás back, I assumed a position of authority. While standing tall and upright, I widened my base and firmly planted my feet into the ground. I puffed my chest forward and placed both hands on my hips. Holding my shoulders back and chin up, I stared vehemently toward the door.

They walked him into the room. He had a smug grin on his face. The grin contained remnants of his previous arrogant expression, following my unexpected collapse. He was likely still feeling accomplished, thinking he had reduced me to a trembling fool. With his ankles chained, he shuffled awkwardly toward me, and as he sat down, I thought, "He doesn't look so scary after all."

I didn't budge. I just stood there, firmly planted in place. I was determined to remain standing in order to exert dominance over him this time. His grin slowly faded as he realized that the person standing before him was not the same one he had left only moments before. He tried

286

to break the silence. "So, you want to know *why*?" He asked in a condescending way.

I didn't speak. I did not react, and I remained expressionless. Instead, I shifted my position and folded my arms in front of me. I just stared ... looking down on him. I'll admit that the silence was awkward, but it accomplished what I had hoped it would; I could sense it was making him uncomfortable. He clasped his hands together in front of him. Resting them on the table, he nervously began to twirl his thumbs in a circular motion. As his body fidgeted in the chair, he refused to hold my gaze. His avoidance tactics reminded me of the uncomfortable old man I had met during Anna's funeral luncheon.

I slowly walked toward him and stopped. I set my palms down on the table before him. Leaning forward, I assertively stated, "No. I don't want to know why. I already know why."

He raised his brows and looked at me. I straightened back up and walked slowly and steadily around the table until I was standing directly over him.

Placing my hands back on my hips, I asked, "Why?"

The inflection in my voice suggested that I was about to answer my own question. I paused for a moment.

Then, in an even stronger voice, I said, "Because *YOU* are a coward."

Satanás looked up at me with complete discontentment on his face. I had struck a nerve. So, as I walked around the table to face him again, I continued.

"Do you know what a coward is, Satanás?" I waited for a response.

He sat in stone-faced silence as I continued, "A coward is nothing more than a bully and a weakling who needs to silence the voices of those he feels inferior to. You picked your victims because you thought they were weak. But in reality, it was *you* who was weak."

I continued, "And, yes, Satanás! That means you are inferior to me and every woman you have ever met. Inferior to all your victims. Inferior to your mother. And even inferior to *Susan*. Remember Susan?"

He startled me as he jumped to his feet, struggling to release himself from the chains. I had done more than strike a nerve. He was downright angry.

"Bitch!" he yelled as he began foaming from the mouth.

The guards rushed over, grabbed him on either side, and forcefully sat him back down in the chair. I smiled a satisfying grin as he writhed back and forth in an attempt to get free.

My eyes pierced through him as I said, "And do you know how cowards are made, Satanás? They have mothers who don't love them and fathers who don't want them. Instead of facing their fears, they are enslaved by them. They are not brave. They are not courageous. They are like little boys who never grew up. On the outside, they try to act tough, but on the inside, they are tiny little crybabies. That is what you are, Satanás—a tiny little crybaby."

Satanás scuffled about in another attempt to get to his feet. But the guards held him firmly in place. He wanted nothing more than to silence me ... silence me the way he had silenced his other victims. His eyes were fuming and fixated on me. He began spewing nasty expletives and spitting all sorts of horrible, rotten names at me. I remained calm and continued to smile, knowing that I was in control.

"You can't silence me, Satanás." And you hate that, don't you? You hate that I am everything that you are not, including free ... free of you ... free of my fears. You are going to hell all alone!"

I continued, "I want you to remember my face. This *is* the face of the one who got away. It is also the face of strength and courage. The face of the one who has shattered *your* world. How does that feel, Satanás? How does it feel to have a woman bring you to your knees?"

I could see the fury seething from his eyes and hear the venom spewing from his tongue. All the while, I chuckled and smiled. I stood my ground firmly, knowing that I had won … as they dragged him from the room.

I left the prison that day with a newfound love of freedom. I had come face to face with my greatest fear … the demon that haunted me for twenty years … the red wolf that visited me in my sleep. In the process of facing my adversary, I had been released from the chains that bound me. And just like that, I could feel freedom everywhere.

I felt it in the winding road I traveled down and in the leaves that were falling from the trees. I felt it in the old Amish buggy parked alone in the shade and in the rolling fields of green. I felt it in the warmth of the sun as it stroked my cheek and in the cool crisp October breeze. I was experiencing a whole new beautiful world … one that was now my reality.

As I continued to drive, windows down, enjoying the fresh clean air, I took my time meandering through the countryside. I spent that time actually taking notice of everything around me. Soaking in the array of colors, it was like a rainbow of nature everywhere I turned. Amber, auburn, crimson, and gold were just a few of the shades that filled the trees and dotted the landscape. Autumn was in full bloom, and with it came the earthy, woodsy smell of the moist ground combined with traces of evergreen. An occasional hint of horse manure wafted in the air, as did the sporadic scents of apples and grapes, ripe with harvest.

Contemplating the events of the past several months, so much had happened and even more had changed. Like a feather carried on a breeze, my life had floated in so many unexpected directions ... directions I never could have imagined. Meanwhile, I had been reminded of the frailty of life and the power of choice. I cringed to imagine that with one slight change in direction or by opting a little different, my whole world would not be the same. I thought about that too, as it may have applied to Anna and all of the other victims.

With that somber thought, my mind fell blank.

Surrounded by empty thoughts, I slowly progressed down the old country road. Aimlessly glancing around as I drove, something strange caught my eye. I hadn't noticed it on my way out to the prison, but there it was, clear as day. I pulled off to the side of the road and stared in disbelief as I read the message. There, in big bold letters painted on the side of an old rustic barn, it read:

Don't just drift along like a feather in the wind.
Be the choice that sets you free.

291

I sat there, just staring, totally speechless. I couldn't believe my eyes. It was as if that message had been put there especially for me.

Just then, the wonderment of the moment was stirred by a cool chill that filled the inside of my SUV. I shivered as my senses were filled with the familiar fragrance of sweet lilacs.

Initially I thought, "Why would I be smelling this, of all things, so far out of season?"

Then, I recalled the lilacs we used to pick in Anna's backyard. Instinct took over as I said aloud, "We got him, Anna. We finally got him."

I sat back and drew in a deep breath of the floral scent that was still lingering in the air. I slowly exhaled and raised my head, looking out toward the sky. I drew in another deep breath. This time, for Anna ... and I smiled.

We were BOTH, finally, at peace.

ACKNOWLEDGEMENT

Special thanks to my daughter-in-law and editor, Kaylene, who took the time to read from beginning to end. With her continued comments, I was able to refine the bare bones of the story and am indebted to her for her insight, assistance, and the little nudges I needed to keep going.

Special thanks go out to my daughter, confidante, and editor, Jessica. Her continued support of this project and so many others has kept me on my toes. Without her constant encouragement, feedback, and assistance, I don't know where I would be today.

Last but certainly not least, thank you to all my family and friends who have provided support of my writings over the years. It is through your encouragement that I am able to fulfill this now unburied dream.

ABOUT THE AUTHOR

Shannon Buckley Moore was born and raised in a small, rural town in Western New York. As a single mother of three, she worked full time while raising her children and earning both her bachelor's degree and MBA.

Early in her career, she served in the United States Air Force. While serving, she won several awards as managing editor of a first-time award-winning Public Affairs Program, Best Hometown News Reporting Program, and Best Small Unit Publication.

Her love of writing continued over the next 40 years, penning both formal and informal content in a variety of styles and formats. Her love of the written word became central to all aspects of her life—personal, professional, and educational. A lifelong learner, when she is not writing, Shannon can be found with any one of her five beautiful grandchildren, who keep her forever young.

www.ingramcontent.com/pod-product-compliance
Lightning Source LLC
Chambersburg PA
CBHW070737180626
46818CB00007B/2884